Frank Black said, "You've seen it, haven't you?"

The question elicited a slow turn of the boy's head.

Frank received a wary, frightened stare.

Behind the viewing gallery's one-way glass, the other members of the Millennium Group exchanged startled glances.

"I've seen it, too," Frank went on with soft matter-of-factness. In his mind's eye, he again glimpsed the last boy, writhing, thrashing. Blood-splattered . . . "I know why you're afraid. But you're safe from it now."

The kid's mouth slowly twisted into an incredulous sneer. "No one is safe from it," he declared, mingling desperation with certitude. "You don't know what you're talking about."

MILLENNIUM

GEHENNA

Look for all the official books
based on the hit Fox television series

MILLENNIUM: *The Frenchman*
MILLENNIUM: *Gehenna*
MILLENNIUM: *Weeds**
The Official Guide to MILLENNIUM*

*coming soon

MILLENNIUM
GEHENNA

LEWIS GANNETT

BASED ON THE CHARACTERS
CREATED BY

CHRIS CARTER

HarperPrism
A Division of HarperCollinsPublishers

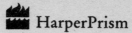 HarperPrism
A Division of HarperCollinsPublishers
10 East 53rd Street, New York, N.Y. 10022-5299

This book contains an excerpt from *Weeds* by Victor Koman.
This excerpt has been set for this edition only and may not
reflect the final content of the paperback edition.

This is a work of fiction. The characters, incidents, and
dialogues are products of the author's imagination and are not to be con-
strued as real. Any resemblance to actual events or
persons, living or dead, is entirely coincidental.

ISBN 0-06-105802-5

HarperCollins®, ®, and HarperPrism®
are trademarks of HarperCollins*Publishers*, Inc.

Cover illustration by Hamagami/Carroll & Associates

First printing: November 1997

Printed in the United States of America

Visit HarperPrism on the World Wide Web at
http://www.prism.com

❖ 10 9 8 7 6 5 4 3 2 1

"I smell blood and an era of prominent madmen."

—W. H. Auden

MILLENNIUM
PROLOGUE

Night falls on the city by the bay. The hills press their flanks up into the dark. Lowland valleys embrace the dark. The water, immense and flat, laps at dark. Downtown office towers bristle at it, among them a pyramid taller than any on earth, a glittering needle of a pyramid. This building punctures the dark—a symbol, for those who weigh such things, of the human ability to challenge night.

The city is San Francisco. There, tonight, darkness presents a particular challenge.

Tonight Gehenna will strike.

MILLENNIUM
CHAPTER

The two BMWs sped from the Haight past Golden Gate Park.

Industrial frat-rock music throbbed in the lead car, the bass lines thundering through the windows, the seats, the floor, through five young men with close-cropped hair. Lars drove. Ralph rode shotgun.

In back, squeezed between Dylan and Nick, Eedo wondered where they were going. What they would do. No one had filled him in on the evening's agenda. "Go for a ride, get high," was all Ralph had said. Eedo didn't feel great about the outing. Under his companions' rowdy cheer he sensed a grimness that contradicted the idea of a night on the town. It was making Eedo increasingly uneasy.

He'd known the others for seven months now, ever since he'd abandoned his old existence as the son of simple Chechen immigrants. Ever since he'd made the fateful step of joining the organization to which one referred, with generic vagueness, as "the Enterprise." Like any twenty-year-old suddenly sure he has found his path in life—a path of glory, shared with guys his own age—he'd trusted his new brothers, seen them as allies, friends.

At first he had. Now Eedo wasn't so sure.

Not at all sure, in fact. He wondered, a knot of tension tightening in his stomach, if this had to do with his performance at work. With its recent slump.

Faith. Discipline. Was he slipping? Was he Enterprise material? Above all, could he work the numbers?

Those questions, their implications, made Eedo afraid.

Streetlights strobed the car's windows. Eedo stared at the road's dipping curves, unwilling to engage eye contact with Dylan on his left, Nick on his right. The rearview mirror occasionally flared the headlights of the BMW following. Like this one, it was new—like this one, full of Enterprise brothers. Guys with faith and discipline. Guys who worked the numbers with brutal efficiency.

It's okay, Eedo told himself. *It's okay. . . .*

Lars slowed the car, pulled over to the curb. The other car drew up behind. Eedo looked out at an expanse of dark grass, black stands of trees. They'd stopped at a park. Auburn Memorial Park and Gardens, Eedo saw on a dimly lit sign by a path that gave entry. Not many people around.

Ralph opened his door, got out, and headed down the path into the park. Eedo watched him merge with foliage, disappear. *What now?* he wondered.

Nick opened a couple of sweating Anchor Steams and passed one to Dylan. They clinked bottles over Eedo's lap, toasting each other, then took covert swigs. It wouldn't do to get noticed by cops, should any be watching the area. Nick leaned into Eedo's ear.

Eedo steeled himself. He knew what was coming.

"Woof!" Nick exclaimed. "Woof-*woof!*"

"Cut it out," Eedo grumbled. This dog

game, the barking, was pushing his buttons. The guys had been going at it since they'd left the barracks. What did it mean?

He didn't want to know, he realized. Nick punched his arm, handed him an Anchor Steam. "C'mon," he said teasingly. "Eedo, we're gonna have a blast."

Eedo took a furtive sip, grateful for the beer's calming effect, and hoped Nick spoke the truth. He focused on the tune blasting from the car's powerful stereo: "*I wanna get high, so high. . . .*"

Lars turned to the boys in back. Eedo studied Lars's smooth baby face, the hardness in Lars's eyes that wasn't babylike at all. "The Dark Prince returns," Lars said slyly. Eedo looked up. Ralph, rematerializing from the park's murk, was striding toward them. A small foil-wrapped packet glinted in one of his hands.

Dark Prince, Eedo thought. *That's on target*. Ralph recently had been made supervisor of the numbers operation. There was a fellow with faith and discipline—Ralph ran his minions ragged. He leaned through the front passenger-side window, handed Lars the foil packet, and said in a deliberate, oddly deadpan tone, "Tickets to the horror show."

Great, thought Eedo.

Lars unfolded the packet. A slip of paper lay within. Perforated paper—the holes formed a grid of squares that resembled a strip of miniature postage stamps. The squares bore no images, however. They were blank, off-white, slightly smudged.

"*I wanna get high, so high, . . .*"

"Yes indeedy," Lars declared. He peeled off four squares and gave them to Ralph, who wheeled away to the second car. Delivering the merchandise, Eedo noted, looking through the rear window. Ralph sauntered back, opened his door, dropped into his seat, and slammed the door hard. Then he retrieved from Lars what remained of the perforated strip.

Lars put the car in gear and shot from the curb.

The car behind followed.

Ralph turned to face Eedo. Slowly, carefully, making sure Eedo had a good view, he tore the paper into its constituent squares.

Acid, Eedo thought, the knot in his stomach twisting tighter. *Blotter LSD, potency unknown, procured from some dealer in a public park.* To Eedo's left, Dylan twitched. To his right, Nick stirred. Eedo wondered if they felt as nervous as he did. If they feared the drug's effect on their mysterious quest. On whatever it was that lay ahead.

Ralph extended a finger to Eedo, the end digit bearing a square.

Eedo looked Ralph in the eyes. They gleamed with amusement. With something else, too. Maybe pity. Or scorn.

Ralph said, "Fetch the paper, Eedo."

Although he had no choice but to do as he was told, for Ralph's word was law, Eedo hesitated. The finger, the square, came closer. Eedo blinked. Then he took the square, put it in his mouth. And chewed.

It tasted dirty. Bitter.

"*Woof!*" Nick yapped in his right ear.

"Grrrrr!" Dylan growled in the left one.

Eedo closed his eyes. He couldn't take the way Ralph was looking at him. The faint smile on his lips. The cold glow in his gaze.

"Good boy, Eedo," Ralph said softly. "You're real good, yes you are."

Twenty minutes later Eedo started to feel the burn. The corrosive buzz. His stomach, twistier now than ever, seemed to digest itself. Eat itself up.

They'd driven to a section of the harbor that was inactive even in daytime, as still as

Stonehenge at night. Piers and warehouses rolled by, dark, gaunt; trash ghosted through the streets, an urban flotsam of newsprint, food wrappers, ragged plastic bags.

Eedo had become much more aware of the bodies flanking him. Of the legs and shoulders penning him in. Tight from the beginning, the squeeze was getting oppressive. Breathing took effort; even the seatback seemed to crowd, to crush from behind. Eedo imagined being caught in a garbage compactor. The image didn't do him good. He tried to make it go away, but it gripped his mind: telling him that close quarters were getting closer, closing in.

The sensation became unbearable. Eedo tried to say something, to alert Lars maybe, tell him to turn off the compactor, flip the switch—anything. *Anything* . . .

But words couldn't escape Eedo's mouth. Nothing could escape this pressure. . . .

The car swung into a tight left turn. The boys in back tilted, rearranging their points of contact, easing somewhat Eedo's sense of confinement. He discovered he could breathe again.

Then he discovered that outside the car, the world was spinning. Left to right. Around and around and around . . .

No, the *car* was spinning—because it was still turning. Lars was driving in a circle. Industrial walls swept by, the headlights streaking them, streaking across a dirty sign that said ACME DRY CLEANING—the headlights rotated these objects around the car. The lights of the other car did the same: turning, turning, painting an encirclement of shabby facades. Eedo felt the pressure again. This turn just wouldn't end. It was locking him into a new, equally horrible crunch.

Abruptly the movement stopped. The boys in back lurched, took a different tilt. Again Eedo could breathe.

But he felt so dizzy. And the windshield was glowing much too brightly. The glass whited out, seemed to melt like something in a science fiction flick. . . .

The cars had stopped face-to-face, Eedo realized. Across a ten-foot divide they now vaporized each other with maximum highbeams.

In the glare the heads of Ralph and Lars showed up as blots that somehow fizzed and crackled around the edges. Ralph's blot said slowly, menacingly, with all the warmth of an alien invader:

"Puppies, it's time to play."

◄◦►   ◄◦►   ◄◦►

*From the roof of the derelict Acme Dry Cleaning
plant—Through a pair of night vision goggles—
Watching—Watching the young men pile out of
the cars—Watching them spill into the fire of
headlights come eye-to-eye—Watching them
stumble giddily, dreamily, through the fire—*

*The face behind the goggles catches a
gleam—A faint gleam, thrown from a window
slamming shut in its door—Faint, but enough to
cast shadow into the pockmarks—Into the pits—
Enough to illumine, just for an instant, the
unearthly gray-yellow pallor—*

Eedo didn't feel on solid ground. The
fusion of the cars' headlights threw quite a
glow, enough to see by, but what Eedo saw
kept shifting. The pavement was shifting—it
felt treacherous, sandy in places, gooey in others. The Acme Dry Cleaning sign looked
insubstantial, even carbonated, as if it were
composed of tiny teeming bubbles. The air
itself was shifting. Mutating. Eedo realized
something that awed him. The air held
numerous mutating substances that he'd never
noticed before—but now could see, taste,
commingle with . . . for the first time. . . .

"Eedo!" someone called, the voice rippling

the air, leaving slipstreams of substance that pulsed here, writhed there. Ancient patterns here—a Chechen carpet, rearranging its nuances midair. Shifting. Going deeper . . . gorgeously deeper. But over there . . . Eedo blinked. He shook his head, stared at the furnace of light between the cars.

His buddies splashed through it like kids at play. Yelling. Laughing at everything, at nothing. They were calling him over. "Eedo, come! Come in the fire . . ."

The fire, thought Eedo. *Purifying fire* . . . The fire that awaited the weak, the infirm. That would incinerate this corrupt, stupid world . . . He staggered toward it, entered it, arms outstretched for balance. Ice-white heat—shifting swarms of light—it felt cold, the fire. Not burning—Eedo moved through unscathed. He took heart from this. He felt deep relief, for the coldness seemed a portent. It told him that, like his companions, he was strong. Worthy. A man of faith and discipline . . .

But wait. His companions—Eedo gaped. They were howling. Barking. Baying like hounds . . . *The dog game*, he thought with a shiver of panic. His panic mutated into something different. Into something like terror.

Because the guys' heads—they were taking nonhuman shapes. Eedo watched them become the heads of dogs. Hellish dogs, howling hellish dogs—their jaws snapped. The fangs gleamed. . . .

They'll eat me, Eedo thought. *Devour me whole*—one of the dog-heads lunged near. Eedo smelled its rank breath, felt a scalding spray of spittle, and suddenly it wasn't a hound coming in for the kill.

It was just one of the guys. Dylan. His buddy Dylan, putting a human mouth to his ear. Whispering, "Hey, man—*run*. Get away while you can."

Eedo saw truth in Dylan's eyes, the urgent truth of a warning. He whispered, "What?"

Dylan didn't reply. He walked away. The others walked away too, out of the lights—human now, a sense of finality in their movements. Eedo watched Lars drain a beer, toss it at a pile of trash, and get in his car. Then the others were getting in the cars. *Time to leave*, Eedo thought. *I'm going with them.*

However, they were slamming doors.

"Wait," Eedo said shakily.

Seven faces looked at him through the windows, eyes stony, knowing. The cars' engines ignited. Then the stereos ignited, sending a throb of bass lines into the night.

"Hey!" Eedo exclaimed.

Both cars backed up with a squeal of tires.

Eedo stood transfixed in lengthening headlight beams, in a welter of bass lines echoing off the dark buildings. The cars stopped, giving him faint hope.

But then one sprang forward, directly toward him. At the last instant it veered, missing Eedo by inches. He broke into a dank, metallic sweat. Now the other car was coming—it also missed, just barely, leaving Eedo weak on his feet, paralyzed with fright. The cars started circling in tandem, like wolves coordinating the torment, the guys leaning out the windows yelling, jeering. Eedo quaked; his mind slid, drained, lost its wits. Headlights and taillights trailed luminous blurs, spinning a vortex that he knew meant death—he had to take Dylan's advice. He had to run.

So he did. In a direction not of his choice, the harrying cars made sure of that. They herded him toward Acme Dry Cleaning. Eedo darted at it, then into it through a crumbled wall, and sought refuge in shadow. His heart pounded. He whimpered, tried to keep a grip on sanity. Behind him the demon cars screamed louder—they were storming the place, Eedo was sure. Seeking the shadow in which he hid.

He bolted and ran deeper within.

*On a catwalk near the high ceiling—Through
the night vision goggles—Watching the terrified
boy flee the sound of the cars—Watching him
make his way by moonlight that seeps through
glass bricks, shattered windows—Watching him
stumble toward his destiny—To the place where
rustwater sprinkles down to the floor—*

Onward Eedo flailed, bumping into
things, slipping on grime, junk. A faint light
glowed further in. Eedo headed to it. He felt
safer now, just a little. The cars' music was
fading. . . . He rounded a corner into a huge
empty space.

Fifty feet overhead a bare bulb dangled,
for some reason lit. Glitter sparkled on the
floor beyond. Cautiously, Eedo approached
the glitter. He found a puddle of discolored
water in which lay shards of glass, fragments
of mirror. A steady sprinkle pattered into it.
Eedo looked up to find the source. The sprinkle descended from a broken pipe. Something
plopped on his shirt. A stray droplet. Rust-
colored, Eedo saw with a start.

Red rain, he thought with fresh fear.

A sound echoed in the dark above. The
pattering sprinkle muffled it. But Eedo was
certain he'd heard something. A soft flapping
noise.

Bats? He stared upward and shuddered. Something gliding there? Hovering?

Watching the boy below—Watching him scan the shadows—Face upturned, pale, afraid— Helpless, weak—Very afraid—

Something flitted up there, Eedo was sure now. Something big. He glimpsed wings. *No, they're much too big.* But yes, wings. Batlike membranes, dipping through the dark. A head poised in between. A head with a snout, a hound's head. Eedo saw a glimmer of jaundiced eyes.

Suddenly the creature dove at him with taloned claws outstretched. Eyes gleaming, the snout baring fangs, hurtling down faster and faster. . . .

Eedo let loose a strangled scream.

Closer—Closer—The boy's eyes go glassy with shock—His mouth opens wider, screaming louder—

Eedo crashed into the puddle as the creature hit, his arms flailing to fend off the talons, the monstrous houndlike snout. To no avail, for the jaw possessed infernal power, as did the talons—a great claw pressed into his chest, driving breath from it. The brilliant yellow eyes glared without pity—portals to damnation, to a damned soul. The snout curled, shivered, and bared fangs; with one stroke it shredded Eedo's upper lip. He shrieked, spattering the snout with blood. It continued to savage him and Eedo writhed, his screams penetrating every shadowed corner.

But there was nothing he could do. And no one who would come to his aid.

The gleaming eyes drew closer. Eedo stopped breathing as they inspected his head, what was left of his mouth. Pincerlike talons forced his jaws open.

Eedo entered a zone of searing concentration. A place where lucidity and horror merge: where lucidity and horror become the same thing. Two talons reached in his mouth. Their tips probed with precision, as if looking for something, and they found it. With extraordinary power, they ripped. They yanked.

Back they came again. Then again.

As the talons used his mouth as a kind of entertainment lounge, one steadily more bloody and plush, Eedo realized something that sent him deeper into the zone of fright. The beast was taking its time. Its methodical, surgical time. No rush. No need to wrap things up quickly.

Eedo would die with excruciating slowness.

Faith, he thought. *Discipline. I've lost them. . . . Now I'm paying the price.*

The beast continued its relentless plucking.

From the darkness above, sprinkle pattered into reddening water.

MILLENNIUM
CHAPTER

2

<hr />

Summer sun filled the garden of the yellow Craftsman-style house. Frank Black descended the porch steps carrying pliers and two large lightbulbs. He walked across neatly trimmed grass to a ladder propped against the house's side. Up it he climbed, to the motion-detector security fixture he'd installed on the roof's fascia board.

It was a good day for this kind of work. Warm, airy, fresh. Fluffball clouds dotted the sky, cotton-white against the blue—no threat from those clouds, at least not yet. Nice weather. Especially for Seattle, city of mist, fog, lashing storms.

"Hey there!" called a voice from below. Startled, Frank turned. Jack Meredith, Frank's next-door neighbor, stood on the lawn, his broad face beaming. "Saw you working up there," he informed Frank. "Putting in a security light, huh?"

Frank smiled faintly. Jack Meredith's early retirement hadn't idled the man. On the contrary, it had given Jack a new career as full-time busybody. "Yeah," Frank said, his voice soft but penetrating. He started screwing in one of the big bulbs. "Days are going to start getting shorter," he continued. "Lights will be nice for Catherine if she comes home from work late."

"Oh," Jack said with interest. "Your wife get her job?"

"Yeah," said Frank, putting in the second bulb.

"Terrific!" Jack exclaimed. "What's the name of what she does again?"

"She's a clinical social worker," Frank said patiently, using the pliers to adjust the mounts. He liked to finish a job well, get it right, down to the last detail. He changed the angle of the lamps slightly. That about did it. A little wiring work was all he had left.

"Oh, right," Jack was saying. "Yeah, sure—clinical social work. Hey, Frank. You got the tools you need?"

Frank cast him an amiable glance. "Jack," he said, "I think I'm squared away."

The front door swung open. Two bundles of energy sped out—Jordan, Frank's five-year-old daughter, and Bennie, Jordan's puppy. Catherine followed more sedately, her face pleasantly oval, smooth, and bright-eyed amid her wavy brown hair. Frank smiled at her. In his austere, weather-honed face, grooves deepened.

"Frank?" she said.

"Yeah?" he replied.

"You've got a phone call," Catherine told him. She said it casually but with an edge. In a way that indicated to Frank the call could be important.

"Daddy!" Jordan yelled as Frank climbed down the ladder. "Did you make it work yet?"

"Almost, honey," Frank said. He stepped onto the grass and stooped to pick up his girl. "What have you been doing?"

"Playing with Bennie," Jordan said happily, her face radiant in the sunshine. "Teaching him tricks!"

"Tricks?" Frank inquired as he carried her back up onto the porch. Bennie followed, snuffling excitedly. "What kind of tricks?"

"Secret tricks," Jordan replied with grave conviction.

"I see," said Frank. "Well, you better not tell me about them, then. If they're secret." He winked at Catherine, handed her their child, and entered the house.

Catherine gazed at the avidly watching Jack Meredith. "Hi," she said with a somewhat perplexed smile.

Jack grinned, pleased that Frank's absence wouldn't put an end to neighborly discourse. "Hi," he said brightly.

The phone lay on the counter that divided the hall from the kitchen. Frank picked it up and said, "Hello?"

A familiar male voice replied through the earpiece, "Hello, Frank? It's Peter Watts."

Frank's grip on the phone tightened. Watts was a member of the Millennium Group, the organization for which Frank did occasional investigative work. "Yes, Peter," he said.

Watts said, "I'm down in San Francisco. I've got what could be a multiple homicide here, possibly something a little more involved."

Something a little more involved. Frank took a deep breath. Behind him, Catherine was entering the house. He didn't want to say anything or do anything that might give her cause for alarm. At the same time, he knew that the "something" Watts mentioned had to be grounds for serious alarm. To Watts he said quietly, "Do you want to send me the details?"

"I could do that, Frank," Watts replied. "But the *lack* of detail has created a high level of concern. I really think we could use you here."

Frank heard Catherine come closer behind him. No question about it now. Watts was on to something. Something that Frank, despite the tang of dread in his gut, knew he had to deal with. "Right," he said. "I'll make the arrangements."

He hung up and turned. Catherine was watching him. Frank gazed back, sustaining eye contact for several long moments, as if to tell his wife that things were okay. But of course, things weren't okay. Awareness of this transferred between them, a wordless understanding born of honesty, tenderness, and a great deal of harrowing experience.

Catherine didn't flinch. She had learned how to deal with these situations. "Was that someone from the Group?" she asked.

Frank nodded. "They've got something for me to look at down in San Francisco."

"Soon?" Catherine said carefully.

Frank moved to the front door, paused there. "Yeah," he said. He turned, resumed contact with Catherine's luminous pale eyes. "Right after I finish up wiring that light."

MILLENNIUM
CHAPTER

3

Frank Black deplaned the shuttle from Seattle at San Francisco International at one fifty-three P.M., a scant three hours following his phone conversation with Peter Watts. He made his way through throngs of tourists, businesspeople, and security checkpoints—the latter ubiquitous now, thanks to the Unabomber and other corroders of daily life—to the car rental counter. No luggage to uncheck. He'd traveled light, as was his custom. The car was waiting for him at the curb.

He drove the expressway into town, then

continued past Golden Gate Park to the
nearby municipal facility that was his destination, Auburn Memorial Park and Gardens.

From his dog-eared San Francisco tourist
guide he'd learned that Auburn Park had
been created in the thirties as a belated
memorial to firefighters who had lost their
lives in the citywide inferno that followed the
Great Quake of 1906. Though modest in
scale compared to Golden Gate—a tiny
patch, really—Auburn had been endowed
with a hefty maintenance fund that the Parks
Department and a semiprivate memorial
foundation administered jointly. The park
therefore had retained its original character
through the fiscal crunches of the previous
several decades. Its charms included a series
of plantings that the public, courted by an
aggessively high-minded outreach committee,
was urged to support in the form of garden
club memberships, monetary donations, and
contributions of time and labor.

The choicest planting was a rose garden,
a tract half the size of a football field, which
in bloom formed a spectacular expanse of red.
The color was intended to evoke fire trucks—
and, alas, the flames that had finished off
what portions of the city the earthquake
hadn't felled.

Having checked other references as well, ones less mainstream than the tourist guide, Frank knew that Auburn Park accommodated pursuits beyond horticulture and the memorialization of civic heroes. At night it served as a staging area for young love, anonymous sex, and drug dealing. The police didn't generally interfere with these activities. No one with a stake in the park's daytime reputation wanted the publicity. Live and let live was the governing philosophy; the nocturnal denizens could go to hell if they wished, as long as they didn't desecrate the gardens.

That, however, had changed.

Peter Watts had faxed Frank some of the particulars, to provide Frank with reading material during the flight down. The material didn't make much sense.

But then, Frank Black and Peter Watts and their colleagues specialized in cases that made no sense.

Following Watts's directions, Frank pulled into the parking lot of Auburn's maintenance center. The lot already held three plainwrap cop cars and four black and whites. Off to the left, beyond a wooden service shed, lay a field of brilliant red blooms—the rose garden, row upon row of neatly tended furrows and bushes. Uniformed and nonuniformed officials slowly moved through the garden, their attire echoing the paint jobs of the parked cars. They were eyeballing the rosebeds. Yellow police-line tape marked off the garden's entire circumference. Outside the tape, knots of onlookers were gathered here and there. Some of these people looked angry, Frank noted.

Volunteer gardeners, he supposed. Well. They had a right to be upset.

He ducked under the tape and strode toward a tall, bald, well-built man with a precisely cropped black mustache—Peter Watts. Near him stood a couple of men, one burly, the other rail-thin, both in street clothes. Frank's practiced eye identified them as SFPD detectives. To Watts he said, "Peter."

Watts turned. "Frank," he said, his eyes betraying a flicker of relief. The two shook hands. "How was your trip?" Watts asked.

"Good," replied Frank. Beyond that one word, he didn't describe his recent experiences or state of mind. Watts and he never wasted time on pleasantries, particularly at a crime scene that merited their attention. The two local detectives, watching with impassive cop-eyes, made no move to be introduced. That was typical. People in law enforcement, if familiar with the Millennium Group, tended

to keep a respectful distance from its members—
no matter how much envy, or fear, might be
in play. Police recognized the seriousness, the
focus that the Group brought to bear. Those
qualities stood out. And provoked a degree of
awe.

"What have you got?" Frank asked Watts.

Watts walked deeper into the garden and
knelt at the base of a rosebush. Frank followed. To him Watts said, "Members of the
gardening club noticed that ashes were being
deposited in the park rosebeds over the past
few weeks."

"Ashes," Frank murmured.

Watts nodded. "This morning," he went
on, "a young woman came here between
seven-fifteen and seven-thirty to do her
weekly stint. She called the police when she
found this." Watts extracted a ballpoint pen
from his windbreaker jacket. He used it to
part the leaves of a decorative shrub that bordered the rosebed. Frank leaned down to get
a look at what leaves had concealed.

Fine gray ashes covered the ground,
freshly deposited, from the look of it. Nestled
in the ash, partially buried, was a human ear.
Just an ear. No head, no skin, no hair—nothing at all to which this fragment of anatomy
formerly had been attached.

Frank sank to his knees to examine it more closely. Ash coated the thing, obscuring its texture and color like an application of makeup. But under the ash, Frank saw blackened edges. This ear had been burned. Scorched, in fact. Basically only the ridged interior portion remained.

A pair of spiders scuttled across it. In the earwell, mandibles flaying, ants feasted on flesh.

Frank stared for several long seconds.

"It appears to be adult," Watts was saying. "A good portion of the interior helix is intact. I think we can get a nice impression from the remaining auricle."

"Yeah," Frank whispered.

Watts said, "There's a lot of ash that's been dumped here, Frank."

"How much?" Frank asked, his mind not on the question.

"We don't know yet," Watts replied. "But preliminary estimates—well. A lot."

"Why here?" Frank muttered.

"What?" Watts said.

"Ashes," Frank said very softly. "Fire . . ."

Watts grimaced at him. Frank was gazing at the ear so intently, he seemed to have lost connection with the rest of the world. This didn't surprise Watts. On the contrary, he'd expected it, for he'd seen it before. He knew from experience that Frank was accessing a reality that no one else present had a prayer of seeing. That perhaps no one else anywhere could see. Still, Frank's concentration—an almost trancelike fix—unsettled Peter Watts. It always had. It always would.

"Fear," Frank said almost inaudibly.

Watts glanced at the detectives. The heavier one, his eyes widening a bit, swallowed. The other one was pretending to check out the crowd control operation around the police line.

Fire . . .

Intense heat . . . Heat glowing through glass . . . Pressed against the glass, staring out, a crazed human face . . . A young man with short hair . . . A mangled mouth . . . A bloodied mouth, missing portions of the lips . . . The boy is screaming. . . . He's in agony, terrified, clawing at the glass. . . . Imprisoned in a fiery hell . . . He's burning alive. . . .

The killer watches him burn. . . .

"Frank," Watts said.

Frank blinked, took a deep breath.

Watts said, "The PD thought the ash could be illegal crematory dumping. But when they looked closer, they realized it had been done with care. Which doesn't make sense. If it's just a random dumping."

"No," said Frank. "He's . . ."

"He?" Watts asked sharply.

"The killer," Frank said. "The killer is . . . "

The screaming kid pounding, pounding against the glass . . .

But the focus shifts. Not on the boy, now. On the surface of the glass itself, shimmering darkly . . .

The glass reflects an image. . . .

The twisted reflection of the killer, watching the boy . . .

Staring at him . . .

Watts was saying, "He's what, Frank?"

Frank closed his eyes, opened them. He turned to Watts and said in a soft, even tone, "The killer knows the victim. He wants to see him suffer."

"Suffer?" Watts asked blankly.

Frank nodded.

"You sure about that?" Watts inquired.

"Oh, yeah," Frank affirmed. "I'm sure."

Watts thought it over. "I think we've got multiple bodies here," he remarked. "Multiple victims."

"Yep," said Frank, glancing at the ash covering the rosebed. The powdery gray stuff bordered the bottoms of bushes as far as he could see.

Watts said, "What's he using? A crematory oven of some kind?" He gestured at the ash. "What could cause that degree of incineration?"

"Maybe a crematory," Frank said. "I can't tell. But I do know this—it's important to the killer that he burns them alive."

Watts took a quick intake of breath. "Why?" he asked.

Frank shook his head. "Don't know," he replied, getting up from his kneeling position. With a heavy sigh, Watts got up too. Both men realized that the detectives had been watching, and listening, for the last few minutes. "Hey," Frank said by way of acknowledgment.

The cops nodded, said nothing.

Watts told them, "I have a call in to a member of our group, a man named Penseyres. If you can help him out with your forensics resources, I think we might be able to get you guys something in the next short while."

"We'll do all we can," the stouter detective replied. He stared at the citizens gathered behind the police line. "You should know," he went on, "that the management of this park is semiprivate. It's not just the city that runs it. Which means we could face complications, in terms of how extensive we get with excavating the . . ." The man paused, gestured at the sizable area in question. "A lot of civic pride," he added. "History, too. The groups involved like to think they keep memories alive."

"Memories of what?" Watts asked.

"The Great Fire back in '06," said the thinner detective. "The fire that started when the city's fuel lines ruptured during the big quake. This place, you might say it's a fire monument. The firemen's union, they take an interest. Politicians take an interest. What I'm saying is, lot of people sure as hell gonna want to know who's putting down cremated remains like . . ." The man took a breath and shook his head. "Like it's some kind of freak burial."

Watts asked, "We'll get interference?"

Both cops shrugged. As if to say, Yeah, it'll happen.

"Then we move fast," Watts declared. "You'll help our man Penseyres?"

The cops nodded. The bigger one asked, "Do you see stuff like this all the time?"

"No," Frank replied quietly, with a conviction that drew searching stares. "Not like this."

Silence descended. It hung palpably in the air, mingling with the scent of rose blossoms, the danker scents of tilled soil, fertilizer, teeming insect life.

Frank broke the silence. He said to Watts, "It might be connected, Peter."

"The killer's sending a message?" Watts speculated.

"He's sending something," Frank said. "What, or why, that I don't know." He moved away, back toward his car.

"We'll be in touch," Watts said to the cops. Then he headed after Frank.

The cops stood there, watching Frank and Watts leave.

"Kind of creeps you out," the thinner one said.

"I can't imagine it," the bigger one remarked.

"No," his companion said. He stooped and brushed aside the leaves covering the ear. "What'd he say? It's important to the killer . . . ?"

"He said," the bigger cop quoted, "'It's important that he watch the victim suffer. That he burns him alive.'"

The two men stared at the scorched ear in the ash. A spider scuttled across it. Both men, hardened veterans with decades of service between them, shivered.

MILLENNIUM
CHAPTER
4

J ordan Black giggled helplessly on her bed. Her puppy, Bennie, was kissing her ear. Kissing her little five-year-old ear with great big wet licks.

"Ooooh!" Jordan squealed with delight. "Bennie, I love you!"

"Grrrlph!" Bennie replied, licking the ear even more thoroughly.

"Okay!" called out a familiar, ringingly authoritative voice. Jordan's mother stood in the doorway with her hands on her hips and a mock-stern expression on her face. "What's going on here?"

Bennie stopped the love treatment. The half-grown border collie looked up at Catherine Black with a tongue-lolling smile, the off-center black spot on his head enhancing the puppy's natural loopiness. Catherine almost cracked up. The dog looked like any child's dream companion. And he felt zero guilt.

"Bennie's giving me kisses," Jordan explained gleefully.

"I see," Catherine said. "Well, there's way too much fun going on in here. It's bedtime. Downstairs for you," she said to Bennie, easing him off the bed.

Bennie trotted to the door, tail aloft and wagging.

"Bye, Bennie!" Jordan called.

Catherine turned to tuck her daughter in. Resuming her mock-authoritarian stance, she said, "And as for *you* . . ."

"Mommy," Jordan interrupted, her voice taking on a thinner, newly serious quality.

"Yes, honey," Catherine said, recognizing this tone.

"When is Daddy coming home?"

Catherine patted Jordan's hand. "I don't know, sweetheart. I'm sure he'll be home soon. Maybe tomorrow."

"Is he working?"

"Yes," Catherine replied.

Jordan said, "Catching the bad man?"

Catherine's heart skipped a beat. She said, mustering up her best effort at serenity, "If there's a bad man, I'm sure Daddy's going to catch him. Now I want you to close your eyes and count as high as you can. Okay?"

"Okay," said Jordan. She closed her eyes and said with fully committed concentration, "One, two, three . . ."

Catherine gazed at her, again awash with interpenetrating emotions. How sweet the child was, how devoted to her parents, her dog. To her cheerful, small world.

"Seven, eight, nine," Jordan steadfastly intoned.

Innocence, Catherine thought. *Is there a way I can help her preserve it?*

"Twelve, thirteen, fourteen . . ."

Catherine blinked back tears. She didn't want to consider the preservability of innocence. Not now, when beholding the real thing blazing from her child. She turned off the table lamp that was the room's main source of light and moved to the door. She'd almost passed through it when the dimness behind her suddenly brightened.

Catherine stopped dead in her tracks. She knew what had raised the room's light level. The brightness came from the windows. From the outdoor security lamp.

She moved quickly to the closest window. Sure enough, at the corner of the house under the roof, the security fixture was burning. It cast a ghostly light across the side yard below. Catherine studied the yard, seeking a moving object, whatever it was that had triggered the motion detector. She saw nothing. Nothing that moved, at any rate. Jordan's wagon, motionless. Gardening implements, motionless. Plants, a table, sundry objects—all motionless.

Really, Catherine told herself. There's nothing there. She felt a little silly. Anxious to get downstairs before she woke Jordan, whose number counting had given way to soft and steady breathing, she started to turn from the window. Out of the corner of an eye she glimpsed something, something subtle, flit through the yard. She froze.

Again she stared through the window. She'd seen something. She *knew* she had— the shadow of something had crossed the yard. A shadow cast by something long and thin. Whatever it was, it had moved quickly. And steadily. With purpose.

Catherine left the room, closed the door, and with quiet haste went downstairs. She considered the possibilities. Something had made that shadow happen.

Bennie looked at her from the bottom of the staircase, head cocked, tail alert. Catherine knelt, put a palm on his back, and whispered, "Is something going on here?"

Bennie stared at her with utter gravity.

"Well?" Catherine demanded. "Yes? Or no?"

Bennie's gaze acquired a soulful dimension.

"Come on," Catherine muttered. She went to a window that looked onto the side yard. The security light was still burning, putting out a quicksilver glow that Catherine realized could play tricks. What with Frank not home, her mind on edge and suggestible. Once more she inspected the yard. Once more she saw familiar, motionless objects.

"I'm making things up," Catherine confessed to Bennie.

"Woof," Bennie said gently, seeming to agree.

Catherine drew down the Roman shade over the window.

Then, very loudly, the phone rang.

Catherine almost jumped out of her skin.

She collected herself as best she could, crossed the room, and picked up the phone. "Hello?" she said guardedly.

Frank's voice said, "Hello, it's me."

"Oh, Frank," Catherine said with a bit of a gasp.

"What?" Frank asked, hearing her unease. "What's wrong?"

"Nothing," Catherine replied. "I just got spooked by the new security light."

"What happened?" Frank demanded. "Are you all right?"

"I'm *fine*," Catherine said emphatically. "It went on and . . . I'm sure it was just a cat. Or something."

Frank said, "I'm sure that's all it was, honey. I'm sure it's just an adjustment. Are you guys all locked up there?"

"We're fine, Frank," Catherine replied. "Really. It's a perfectly safe neighborhood."

"Of course it is," her husband said reassuringly. Catherine heard someone call his name from the background. He said, "Can you hold on a second?"

"Yes," said Catherine, hoping her heart rate would calm.

Moments later Frank said, "Something's come up and I've got to go. Do you want me to call you back?"

"No," she said.

"Are you sure? You've got a couple of hours before bedtime."

"Yes. I'm sure. Frank?"

"Yeah?"

"Did you catch the bad man?"

A second or two passed. Then Frank said, "Not yet. But we will."

"I know," Catherine told him.

"Bye, Catherine," he said. "I love you."

"I love you too," she replied.

"I'll call you tomorrow," he said, concern evident in his voice. "Get some sleep, all right?"

"I'll do that," she said. "Bye."

She hung up, missing him keenly.

Bennie was giving her a slightly worried stare.

MILLENNIUM

CHAPTER

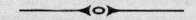

It was nine forty-five in the Enterprise dorm. A quarter hour to lights out. Dylan lay on his bunk, eyes closed, trying to ignore the clamor that filled the long, high-ceilinged room.

Until recently Dylan had enjoyed this part of the evening. It was the sole time in his daily routine not devoted to labor of one kind or another. Three kinds of labor, actually. The physical workouts of the drills. The mental grind of the education sessions. And most draining by far, the rote labor of working the numbers.

There was a fourth kind too, an umbrella category that included the others. Dylan thought of it as labor of simple survival: what it took to stay alive here.

A big workload, all in all. With only an hour of free time to leaven it, nine to ten. A period to do whatever you wanted before hitting the sack. Take a shower, read comics, just think; but, of course, no TV. Which didn't matter; by nine everybody was glazed over anyway. No one needed TV.

Dylan listened to neighborhood chatter, babble from nearby bunks, the few voices he could make out against the room's background din. He'd heard it all before, in variations or verbatim. Lars describing the dissection of internal comubustion engines. Nick babbling about the jazz concert he'd attended his last night off. Dylan had listened to every detail of that concert at least five times. So had everyone else within earshot of Nick's bunk. Didn't it strike anybody as a little strange?

Besides himself, Dylan feared it did not. He feared even more his growing anxiety about pre–lights-out in the dorm. It had mounted over the previous few days, this anxiety. Ever since his last night on the town.

Ever since his final night with Eedo Bolow. Dylan opened his eyes and stared at the iron springwork of the bunk above him. That bunk was vacant now. No one read magazines on it, or cracked jokes from it, or used it as a platform to unfurl expectations for the future. Not anymore, during the hour of babble between nine and ten.

One empty bunk up there. Eedo Bolow's.

"Damn you," Dylan muttered at the rusty springwork. He rubbed his eyes, thinking the obvious and hating it: There was no need to add to Eedo's damnation. That pretty well had been taken care of already.

Dylan checked his watch. Nine forty-eight now. Twelve minutes to go.

Three guys, new ones in their teens, walked by naked but for towels around their waists, fresh from the showers. Dylan didn't know their names. He wondered when someone new would be assigned the bunk overhead. An eager recruit with dreams of fast cars, wealth, a limitless future. Yet another kid cut off from his past, irrevocably ripped from everything he'd known before. *Like me,* considered Dylan. *Like the rest of us here.* And like the rest of us, running the serious risk of not making it through. Of failing. Losing faith, discipline.

That had happened to Eedo. And it could happen to me, Dylan thought bleakly.

Nine fifty-two. Dylan reached under his

mattress for the vial that held his stash of
pills. He used them sparingly, for they technically were banned. Lately, though, they'd
been extra-useful, for they guaranteed dreamless sleep. In other words, seven straight
hours of no Eedo Bolow.

Dylan considered what then would come,
with the start of a new day.

At five sharp the bells would rouse him,
would launch him into a massive scramble of
dozens of young men donning workout uni-
forms. That was a good place too, early morning—a blur of breakfast and vigorous drills.
Too busy to be haunted by Eedo.

Then came the prelunch education session. A wonderful place, that session. A loud
place, wild and scary and inspirational, no
room for distractions, lurid as it was with
visions of hellfire consuming the planet. Eedo
didn't stand a chance of barging in there.

Then lunch. Sweaty guys shoving high-
carb junk into their faces, minds in apocalyp-
tic afterglow, in thrall to smoldering ashes,
the End. Another no-entry for Eedo.

Then the afternoon education session:
tales of riches and power! The bounty of shattered civilizations, flowing to the righteous.
To the virile, the pure, the young—in other
words, to the Brothers of the Enterprise. All

the guys loved that. Dylan was no exception. So fuck you, Eedo, don't even think about it. You lost out on riches and power. Because *you* are *dead*. That's right. Dead!

Then, immediately after riches and power, the mandatory showers, which always came as such a relief. Plenty of shampoo and soap and thick clean towels, the guys gleeful in the steam-filled room, images of glory racing through their heads. Mass nakedness, fraternal bonding.

Then the sober-up time, the quick hustle into fresh T-shirts and jeans, locker doors banging, deodorant spraying, not a whole lot of talking. Focus-time. It led to the most important part of the day, the boiler room session. The highest arena for proving faith and discipline:

Working the phones. Working the numbers.

The numbers, Dylan thought nervously. He used to excel at that. The last few days, though, every now and then Dylan had found himself drifting in the boiler room. Not as concentrated as he should be.

Then, after dinner and the postdinner videos, the free period. Nine to ten: Dylan's new low point. Unlike every other part of the day, it offered few defenses against fearful speculation. Unstructured, no focus, nothing really to do. It just opened the floodgates.

"Damn you," Dylan hissed at the bunk above.

Nine fifty-six. Time to pop the sleeping pill and wait for numbness to banish the mystery that was haunting him:

Eedo's ear.

It shouldn't have survived. It should have been reduced to fine ash, just like the rest of the body. But it hadn't. Why?

Dylan had been asking himself that question since day before yesterday, when he and two others, under cover of early morning darkness, had distributed what was left of Eedo Bolow in the rosebeds of Auburn Memorial Park and Gardens.

During that ritual, Dylan had reached into the plastic-lined burlap sack, expecting to find nothing but floury powder. Then his hand closed on something that felt like a dried half-pear. He pulled it out, saw what it was. The other guys, eager to get going, didn't see him make the discovery.

And Dylan didn't say anything about it. He had his reasons. The chief of which concerned the fact that he'd found the left ear.

Not the right-side one. The left one.

Dylan harbored a theory about the significance of this. But he scarcely could think it through. Was he going nuts, making things up—guilty of the same foolishness he'd once seen in Eedo? Or had Eedo been on to something all along?

The whole mess derived from a couple of stories that Eedo had told months before.

Back in Chechnya, the part of Russia where Eedo was born and raised through his early teens, religion played a big role in everyday life. God played a big role. Eedo got off on all that then. He even did a stint as acolyte in the local church, assisting at Orthodox Mass dressed up in robes and regalia. So it was a major deal when the district bishop, making rounds at Eedo's little church one Easter Sunday, presented him with a gold crucifix on a chain. Eedo wore it around his neck—"religiously," he'd said with a smile—for two or three years.

Then his parents moved the family to the United States and everything changed. Eedo swiftly lost interest in church. Much to his mother and father's dismay, he developed a liking for pot, fast girls, easy money. He hung with crowds that gradually got wilder.

His fashion evolved accordingly. He snipped off the crucifix's chain, turned the cross into an earring, and wore it until he turned twenty-one.

On his left ear.

Of course, joining the Enterprise meant

saying good-bye to earrings and leather and chrome chains, all the paraphernalia of Eedo's late adolescence. The Enterprise favored a clean-cut look—it was nothing if not military in its organization, style, and aims. Joining it was like entering boot camp: Shave your head, get rid of old identities, embrace a new outlook. A kind of conversion experience. Not a halfhearted one, either, you definitely had to go all the way.

So for multiple reasons, Eedo's earring had to go. It didn't bother him, needless to say, he had a good attitude—hey, if you're going to convert, you *convert*. End of story. Don't ask questions. Don't look back.

Still, Eedo made some remarks about the subject that stuck in Dylan's mind. Just a few remarks; but they seemed so peculiar. Dylan now wished he'd never heard those words. He knew they were the root cause of his declining performance with the numbers. His distress during the free hour between nine and ten.

The dorm was quieting. Dylan looked at his watch. Ten o'clock sharp. At the room's other end Ralph was going bunk to bunk, making the body count. Dylan composed himself, tried to smooth worry from his face; Ralph had been keeping an eye on him lately. Especially in the boiler room.

Luckily the pill was taking effect.

Ralph paused by Dylan's bunk. "You okay?" he asked.

"Just fine," Dylan replied sleepily.

Ralph moved on. Dylan settled into his bunk, feeling tendrils of numbness spread through his mind. Ralph knows I'm cracking, he told himself. However. He doesn't know about the ear.

But Dylan could relax now. He even could ponder, briefly, in the few minutes he had before blankness overtook him, the memories that so unsettled his existence.

He and Eedo had joined the Enterprise at the same time. They'd shared the double-decker bunk from the start, Eedo on top, Dylan on bottom. Occasionally, during the free hour, they would exchange comments about the thrilling but scary world in which they both were initiates—a commonality they soon lost, but which for a time bonded them quite closely. It was during such a talk that Eedo told Dylan about the crucifix earring.

Eedo mentioned it because the now-naked ear was developing a funny sensation. It felt as if the earring somehow were coming back—growing back. Of course, it wasn't. But the feeling didn't go away.

Instead, it got stronger. Eedo attributed

this to some kind of effect in his brain, akin to the phantom-limb sensation that amputees experience. He tried to ignore the sensation.

But it scared him. Badly enough that he couldn't keep it to himself. So he told Dylan about it.

"The feeling gets intense when I'm near the Leader. When he's around, it feels totally real. And if he looks at me—or worse, speaks to me—it hurts. No shit, Dylan. The fucking earring is *there*, and it *hurts*."

Dylan hadn't taken this seriously. "You're making things up," he'd remarked with a laugh. "Spooking yourself. Just let it go."

But now Dylan couldn't let it go. Not after having found the very ear in question. Weirdly, inexplicably intact.

A sign? A sign of what?

Or was he simply losing his mind?

Dylan lay on his bunk asking himself those questions, but without feeling the dread that the questions brought to the boiler room, the free hour. In his head, the tendrils of numbness were fattening nicely—taking up more and more space, merging into big blank chunks where nothing ticked and nothing tocked.

At this point, to his great relief, Dylan couldn't feel much of anything at all.

MILLENNIUM
CHAPTER

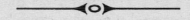

The San Francisco Police Department's Forensics Division occupied a suite of rooms in the downtown Hall of Justice. The centerpiece of the facility, a large lab, held an array of advanced technology, instruments capable of identifying the composition, integrity, and history of virtually any physical object. Skilled technicians tended the lab during daytime hours, filling it with professional bustle and a spectrum of high-tech sounds—the hums, whirs, and whines of inquisitive machines. At night, however, the lab generally was a quiet place. Such was the case at ten twenty-three when Frank Black, sitting at a desk in the middle of the room, caught himself once again staring at the phone.

He couldn't get his wife and daughter off his mind. Nor did he want to get them off his mind. How could the new security light have so spooked Catherine? It was just a light. Had she seen or heard something that she didn't want to mention? Something alarming—but not sufficiently alarming to pass on to her husband? But that wasn't like Catherine. She and Frank kept very little from each other. Still, Frank supposed that she might hesitate to tell him about an experience derived more from nerves than from a real event. Then again, suppose there had been some event, one Frank should know about, but which Catherine wasn't convinced really had happened? Might she have held back because she didn't want to bother him with a false alarm? When in fact it wasn't a false alarm?

Circular thinking, Frank told himself. Around and around to no good end. Probably Jack Meredith set off the light. Anyway, Catherine always had Bennie to protect her and Jordan. Frank smiled at the idea. Bennie, fierce guard dog.

Someone knocked on the hallway door.

Peter Watts, who was sitting at a light table going over photos of the Auburn rose garden scene, went to the door and opened it. A middle-aged man pushed in a handtruck piled with sealed cardboard boxes. Frank rose and approached him.

Watts said, "Frank, this is Jim Penseyres. He worked at VICAP just after you left. I don't know if you ever met."

Frank shook Penseyres's hand and said, "No. Hi."

Penseyres had the full, genial face of a Midwesterner, one lacking the austerity of Frank's features or the nattiness of Watts's trim mustache. To Frank the man resembled a youngish Gerald Ford—solid and undistinguished. Yet Penseyres radiated a quiet, intelligent authority. Frank didn't doubt that he possessed those qualities, and more. The Millennium Group chose its members too carefully.

"What did you find?" Frank asked with a glance at the cardboard boxes.

Penseyres said, "The excavation of the site is incomplete pending a problem with the Parks Department, but I think we were able to separate out most of what there was in the plant beds." With a cutter he slit the seals of the box on top. He pulled the flaps open, revealing a sizable quantity of fine, dark-gray ash. "Thirty-nine pounds of carbonized human remains," Penseyres was saying. "Roughly the equivalent of seven adults. Dating is difficult, but there appeared to be a defined stratum, which would indicate more than one deposit."

"Seven people turned to dust," Watts remarked.

"At least seven," said Penseyres. "Like I mentioned, we have a problem with the Parks Department. Seems *they* have a little problem with the historical society that co-administers Auburn Park. The society wants a special investigation. So there's a dispute over jurisdiction, and a delay in collecting whatever may still be at the site."

"Anything else?" Frank asked.

"The remains are clean," Penseyres replied. "By that I mean uniform, no large fragments, apart from the partial ear. Which would indicate extreme heat."

"Yeah," Frank said, staring at the ash. Quite extreme, he thought. About as extreme as heat gets. . . .

The face against the glass . . . Eyes blazing terror, his hair smoking . . . Curling, melting . . . A hand pounds the glass with a final spasm . . . Death throes . . . Lifelessly, the hand slides down the glass . . .

Frank blinked, and exhaled. Penseyres and Watts were regarding him with interest. Frank asked Penseyres, "What kind of heat are we talking about?"

"Bone carbonizes at fourteen hundred degrees," Penseyres said evenly. "But I'd put this at twenty-one, twenty-two hundred."

Frank nodded. Something was bothering him. He remembered. And said, "What about the ear?"

Penseyres shrugged. "Shouldn't have survived," he said.

"But it did," Frank remarked, half to himself.

"Good thing, too," Penseyres said with a satisfied grunt. From a pocket he extracted a plastic evidence bottle. Clear solution filled it, giving a preservative bath to the semi-charred, now ash-free, ear. "I don't know how it survived," Penseyres went on. "But we pulled an impression and . . ." He paused, eyes gleaming both with satisfaction and a degree of perplexity. "Something else, too. Something just as lucky."

"What!" Watts demanded.

"The tissue contained traces of lysergic acid," Penseyres said quietly. "LSD. Also traces of phosgene, a relatively uncommon gas best known as a by-product found at accident sites. Most commonly at chemical plants using carbon tetrachloride."

Frank said, "Dry cleaning fluid."

Penseyres nodded. "There was an accident at a big dry cleaning facility here seven years ago. They've got a block of abandoned buildings down near Pier Twenty-three."

Frank glanced at Watts. "Want to take a look?"

Watts checked his watch. "It's ten-thirty, Frank. What can we find now that we won't find tomorrow?"

Frank shrugged. "Who knows? I have a feeling about this." He grabbed his jacket and moved to the door.

F rank drove. Peter Watts rode shotgun.
A steady rain fell, depriving the city of
moonlight, rendering the night damply thick.
Appropriate conditions, Watts supposed, for
visiting a defunct dry cleaning facility.

The two men didn't talk a lot during the
fifteen-minute trip to the gritty industrial district surrounding Pier Twenty-three. Both
were thinking through the facts they'd gathered concerning a minimum of seven inciner-
ated human beings. So far the facts didn't add
up to much. From a cold-eyed perspective,

one not taking into account the visions that
the ashes had conjured for Frank, the facts
didn't even indicate the certainty of homicide, or any other serious crime. But neither
Frank nor Watts doubted they confronted
one of the most difficult challenges of their
careers. Frank because his mind's eye had
glimpsed senseless cruelty, senseless evil;
Watts because he trusted Frank's take, and
also because he found something fundamen-
tally perverse about embellishing a monument to firefighters with the ashes of roasted
murder victims.

"There it is," said Frank, pointing at a
dingy sign on the side of a large dilapidated
building.

"Acme Dry Cleaning," Watts read from
the sign. "Crisp silk and pressed suits."

"Once upon a time," Frank murmured.
He turned onto an entry lane that led to an
ample, badly paved court well away from the
street. Gaunt warehouses, chain-link fences,
loading docks, and the dry cleaning plant
bordered the court. The only illumination
came from security lights shining at an angle
from one of the warehouses. The other buildings, almost as dark as the night itself, looked
to have been abandoned long before.

Frank parked in the court's center and

turned off his headlights. The court's gloom deepened; rain thrummed onto the car, the pavement, the lifeless buildings.

Both men got out of the car with lit flashlights. The two beams crossed swords as they played over Acme's crumbling facade. Frank and Watts headed for it, shoulders hunched against the downpour.

They didn't need a door to gain entry; a portion of the front wall had shattered. Frank paused just inside, turned, and used his flashlight to scan the pavement they'd come across. The beam settled briefly on a beer bottle lying on a patch of sodden newprint and then moved on to probe the outlines of what lay ahead. Watts's beam scouted the floor. There had been an accident here, all right. The place looked like the casualty of a war zone. Seven years after fire had gutted it, the stench of scorched metal and wood still lingered.

Frank moved in slowly, avoiding puddles, tarry patches of oil, smashed bits of mortar work and machinery. Watts followed. Their beams advanced before them, finding few signs of recent human activity. Some ancient cigarette stubs, a stained sweater hung improbably on the knob of a door that led nowhere, and a faint reek of urine. Very faint.

If homeless people encamped here, none had done so recently. Collapsed walls created slopes of debris. Piles of rusty pipes and plastic tubing indicated a degree of salvage work, halfhearted at best. Rain pattered through broken clerestory windows high overhead.

"Not much of anything left," Watts commented. His tone suggested little confidence they would hit pay dirt.

"No," Frank admitted. But he cocked his head, as if sensing something. He probed deeper with his flashlight and walked farther in.

Watts hesitated, then followed.

Frank said, "Peter, do we know who owns these buildings?"

"The city," Watts replied. "They've been for sale for years. No buyers, though."

They walked past a bank of charred electrical transformers, glass crunching underfoot. A small creature fled their approach, a rat or a mouse. "I see light," Frank announced. "Around the corner up ahead."

Watts slipped on something and cursed.

"You all right?" Frank inquired.

"Just shining my shoe," Watts replied. "On a dead animal. I think a cat." He peered in the direction Frank was indicating. A soft glow seeped from the edge of a partition that went ceiling-high. "What the hell's the power source?" Watts muttered. "Don't tell me this wreck still has juice?"

"The light could be coming through a window," Frank said, moving on toward the partition.

Behind it stretched a large open space. Forty or fifty feet above floor level, a bare bulb burned. Near it a thin waterfall poured from somewhere on high, from a ruptured pipe or a leak in the roof; it spattered down through increasingly dim air to the floor, into puddles that held glittering shards of glass. Rust-colored puddles, Frank noted. Distinctly reddish. Fragments of shiny glass scattered around.

With his flashlight he probed the ceiling, trying to pinpoint the water's source. The spray diffused the bulb's light, creating a gauzy glare that ran interference with Frank's beam. He couldn't make out much beyond the bulb. Spiderwebs of catwalks near the ceiling. Girders, rafters, machinery mounts . . .

The catwalk in a shadowed corner . . . a presence up there? Someone, or something, watching from it?

"I don't know, Frank," Watts was saying. "What do you think they'd be doing in here?"

Frank looked down, at water falling in reddish puddles. Smaller droplets pattered; heavier ones plopped. A half-submerged slab of glass caught Frank's eye. Like a mirror it reflected the gauzy light high overhead, the shadowed dimness behind the light. Frank said quietly, "Maybe this is where . . ." He paused; he could feel something coming. He could *see* it coming, in the reflective slab of glass:

Hurtling down on wings, the face inhuman . . . Open jaws . . . Fangs gnashing with demonic power . . . Gnashing at a terrified young man . . . Mauling the boy's face . . . Lacerating his lips, his mouth . . .

Frank realized something. He'd seen that face before. Burning behind thick glass.

"This is where they did what?" asked Watts.

Frank said, "Maybe this is where the victims were subdued." He gazed up at the falling water, at the shadowed catwalk beyond. He listened to droplets hitting, to the patter and plop of reddish drizzle. *Bloody rain*, he thought. The idea hit him hard:

The terrified guy on the floor . . . Flailing in red puddles, the same kid who burned behind a window . . . Trying to fend off the beast . . . The thing gnashes at his face, his mouth. . . . Unearthly fangs in an unearthly houndlike snout . . . Red rain falls on the boy, on the beast, on the puddles . . . A downpour from hell . . .

Frank played his flashlight across the floor. He moved on, sensing the presence of something else here. To his left he saw a fleck of white. A small white object. Several small white objects, scattered in a shallow pool.

"Peter," Frank said, heading to the puddle. He leaned down for a closer look. Watts joined him.

They were looking at five human teeth.

"Freshly yanked, I'd say," Watts commented, pointing out a filmy fragment of tissue floating on the puddle's surface. "Within the last several days."

Frank nodded grimly.

"Nice way to subdue a victim," Watts continued. A fat droplet splattered on his head's hairless topside. With a hand he wiped off the moisture; and stared at a sepia gleam on his fingers. "Christ," he whispered. "Dilute blood?"

"Rust," Frank said. "But the color evokes blood." He gestured at the spray pattering down around them, and added in a steelier tone, "The victim suffered over a protracted period of time. The killer set it up that way, carried it out that way. The burning was just the climax."

Watts extracted a pair of tongs from his jacket and used them to slip the teeth into an evidence bag. He said, "Red rain at the scene of a catastrophic fire. Whose ritual would that be?"

Frank thought about batwings. About the suggestion of a powerful snout, the preternaturally gnashing fangs. "Can't say," he replied. "It's the ritual of something I've never seen before. Something inhuman, Peter."

"A psycho?" Watts asked.

"No. This isn't the inhumanity of a crazed human being. It's beyond human. Not human."

Watts rose with a grunt, the teeth-gathering done. "SFPD will love it," he declared.

Frank didn't comment. He was listening to the plops and patters of falling blood.

"You want to stick around?" Watts asked.

"No," Frank said. "I want to get out of here."

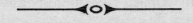

At five o'clock sharp, bells blasted in the Enterprise dorm. Like an automatic alarm, as certain as sunrise, the sound jump-started each day, goading dozens of young men from sleep to full wakefulness in an average of less than six seconds. This day was no different; bare feet slapped the floor en masse. No different but for one exception. Ralph, patrolling the aisles, noticed it right away.

For some reason, the bells hadn't penetrated Dylan's brain. Ralph shook Dylan's shoulder. "C'mon," he said loudly, eliciting stares from the immediate surround. The pulling-on of pants slowed; the buttoning of shirts paused. "Dylan!" Ralph bellowed. Murmurs spread up and down the aisle, and to adjacent aisles, as more and more men realized something was amiss.

Ralph slapped the unresponsive face. Dylan's eyes flew open. He said clearly, without hesitation, "It hurts."

"Hurts?" Ralph demanded.

Dylan nodded with vigor.

"Get up," Ralph ordered. "Now!"

Dylan sat up, then got to his feet. "Sorry," he mumbled as he groped for his pants. "I—uh. I guess I was dreaming."

"Everybody's staring," Ralph snapped. "Staring at you."

"Yeah. I'm sorry."

"What do you think they're thinking, Dylan?"

"I don't know. I don't know."

"They think you're a loser, that's what. This isn't a dream. You got that? No dream."

"Sure, Ralph. I got it. No dream."

Ralph's face pressed closer. He said in a low tone, "What's the matter with you?"

"Nothing," Dylan muttered. "I'm fine. Really. I am."

But he wasn't fine. The contempt in Ralph's eyes told Dylan that. As did the sour fright in Dylan's stomach. Oh shit, he thought. Even sleep wasn't safe anymore. He really had been dreaming—with an intensity that had blocked the bells. Completely blocked the noise, as though he'd been sealed in a soundproof room.

At eight-eleven Frank Black was sitting in a breakfast joint sipping coffee and reading the *Chronicle*. The rose garden discovery had made the front page:

CREMATED HUMAN REMAINS FOUND IN PARK
EVIDENCE OF MASS HOMICIDE?
COMMITTEE CALLS FOR
PRIORITY INVESTIGATION

The story didn't mention the Millennium Group. No surprise there. The group took pains to limit publicity about its activities. So did the various law enforcement agencies that the group assisted; generally the police didn't have a problem with taking credit for solving tough cases, especially when someone with Frank's talents played a role. By-the-book procedure looked more professional than did paranormal detection, any day.

That suited Frank just fine. The less the public knew about what he did, the less trouble his family would encounter. Catherine and he already had endured their fair share of unwelcome attention. And more. Frank caught himself brooding about the stalker. The Polaroids. The nightmare that had ended his FBI career. And very nearly had ended his marriage, the bedrock of his life.

He got up, went to a pay phone, and called home. Jordan answered. "Hello?" she said, her voice morning-bright.

Frank smiled. With a playful growl he said, "This is Detective Hound from the Seattle Zoo. I've just gotten reports of a young lady teaching her dog secret tricks—"

"Daddy, Daddy, Daddy!" Jordan cried.

"How are you, sweetheart?" Frank asked warmly.

"Wonder-*full*," Jordan replied. "Where are you?"

"San Francisco, honey. Not too far."

"Is *that* where he is?" Jordan inquired.

"Who?" Frank asked. "Who are you talking about, Jordan?"

"The bad man," Jordan said.

Frank winced. He hadn't expected this question. "As a matter of fact," he told his daughter, "I'm looking for a good man. A man who will help me."

"What for?" Jordan asked with interest.

"Find a present for a little girl who lives in Seattle."

"Oh!" Jordan exclaimed. Then she said a trifle scoldingly, "Can't you do that by yourself?"

Frank laughed. "I guess I could. Can I talk to Mommy?"

"Yes," Jordan said. "Daddy—when are you coming home?"

"I hope tomorrow. Bye, sweetie."

Catherine's voice came on the line: "Tomorrow, I take it?"

"Yeah," said Frank. "Probably tomorrow. Everything okay?"

"Of course," Catherine said calmly. "Last night's little scare—I wasn't used to the light, that's all. Frank, I'm sorry about you-know-what."

"Jordan's question about the ___?"

"Uh-huh."

Frank said, "For the record, darling, I'm looking for a good man. In case it comes up."

"Any progress, Frank?"

"Some. We're getting there. Not as fast as I'd like, but we are making progress."

"Good," Catherine said cheerfully, as much for Jordan's benefit, Frank knew, as for his. "Well, we have to finish up breakfast here and get on with things. Thanks for the call, Frank. I love you."

"Me too!" Jordan squealed in the background.

"Love you both," Frank said. He hung up and went back to his booth. To the *Chronicle*, the park story, the now-tepid cup of coffee. Frank drained the cup and ordered another.

At nine sharp he entered the forensics lab. There he found Peter Watts gazing through the lens of a large, lighted magnifying instrument.

"Frank," Watts said by way of greeting.

"Morning," said Frank. "What do you have, Peter?"

With a gesture Watts invited him to check out the magnifier. Frank looked through the glowing lens. It was trained on a crowned, somewhat discolored tooth.

Watts said, "The number sixteen molar has a crown that was done more recently than the other work." He used a dental scraper to indicate the crown.

Frank studied the tooth and asked, "Any indication how it was removed?"

Watts said, "From the scoring in the enamel it looks like some kind of crude metal tool."

Frank nodded grimly.

"There's a cuspid filling here that's pretty much state-of-the-art," Watts continued. "The other fillings are substandard compound amalgam, which indicates something important." Watts crossed to a light table that displayed black-and-white X-ray blow-ups.

"They were done somewhere else," Frank said, moving to the light table.

Watts nodded. "There are two root canals done with a process known as N2. They look different here in the X-rays."

Frank looked at the gray cores of the images of the teeth. They did in fact reveal minute differences in texture.

Watts said, "You'll see this kind of work coming out of Eastern European countries, out of Russia. I think the poor general condition of the teeth would suggest the latter."

"Who's running this through records?" Frank asked.

"Penseyres," Watts replied. "He's working with the PD on it."

The hallway door opened. Penseyres entered and said, "Got a surprise for you guys."

Frank and Watts knew the man who followed Penseyres through the door. His name was Mike Atkins. He was a bit older than the others, with a thick head of white hair, and of somewhat smaller physical stature, but his presence projected no less formidably. The lab's antiseptic atmosphere acquired a new charge as he took in the room, its occupants. Watts and Frank approached him with welcoming smiles.

"Look who came down from the mountain," Watts said, shaking Atkins's hand. "What are you doing here, Mike?"

Atkins said wryly, "I caught the same fish three days in a row. Big, brown. Five, five and a half pounds if he's an ounce. Figured the fish and I both needed a day off."

That got chuckles from Atkins's Millennium Group colleagues. He extended his hand to Frank; they exchanged a firm shake. "Hey, Mike," Frank said with feeling.

"Good to see you," Atkins said. "Thanks for coming on such short notice."

"It's some case," Frank remarked. He and Atkins maintained steady eye contact.

"Yeah," Atkins said. A brief silence filled the lab.

Penseyres cleared his throat and said, "We just need a break on these dental records."

"Frank," Atkins said. "You have a second?"

"Sure," Frank said.

The two men left the room.

MILLENNIUM
CHAPTER

9

Frank Black and Mike Atkins ambled out of the Hall of Justice and down the sidewalk, dodging a stream of excited schoolkids let loose on recess. Neither man felt a need for immediate talk. Frank knew what was on Atkins's mind. He didn't know the details, however; and anticipated them with a mixture of keen interest and dread.

Atkins paused near a shaded public drinking fountain. From his jacket pocket he removed an envelope. For a moment he stared at traffic passing by. Then he locked

eyes with Frank and said, "I never told anyone about these, as you'd asked. But I want
you to know I was very upset when I opened
the package and saw them. I can only imagine how you must have felt."

"Right," Frank said tonelessly. He took the
envelope from Atkins, opened the unsealed
flap, and extracted a number of Polaroid photos.
He looked at each one in quick succession;
they all featured Catherine and Jordan. In a
grocery store parking lot, loading the van
with full brown bags. Outside Jordan's kinder-
garten, dropping her off and picking her up.
Entering the yellow house.

"I appreciate you confiding in me," Atkins
said.

Almost imperceptibly, Frank sighed. He
said, "You're the reason I was even able to
come back to work, Mike. That I'm a member of the Group."

Atkins nodded, absorbing every expres-
sive nuance in Frank's face. He asked, "Does
Catherine have any idea yet these new photos were taken?"

Frank shook his head. "I never like to
keep anything from her. . . ." He paused, not
knowing how to put this. Then he said,
"We're barely settled in."

"You were right not to," Atkins said.

"That's your threat assessment?" Frank asked.

With quiet authority Atkins said, "There's a low risk potential in the photographer escalating from the stalking phase. It's been three years since his first mailing and he's still keeping a safe distance. He doesn't want to be discovered."

"Even though he's followed us to Seattle," Frank pointed out.

Atkins said, "I'd be more concerned if I thought this was really about Catherine or your daughter."

"What do you mean?" Frank asked with surprise.

"He sends the photos to you, Frank. The envelopes have your name on them."

Frank stared at Atkins, his eyebrows tensed.

"What's the object of terrorism?" Atkins asked rhetorically.

"Terror," Frank said.

"That's all he wants at this point."

"Then he's a success," Frank declared. "Did you get anything else, Mike?"

Atkins shook his head. "The film was purchased in the state of Washington. Beyond that, he was very careful not to contaminate the film or the package with anything I could pull."

Frank's shoulders sagged a touch. Atkins noted this, and returned Frank's gaze. Frank said in a probing tone, "You come all the way out here just to allay my fears, Mike?"

Atkins said bluntly, holding nothing back, "It'd be the easiest thing in the world for you to go home and be with your family right now, Frank. But we need you out here on this one. We need your abilities. I've got a bad feeling about this case." Atkins lifted his chin. "And I'm sensing you do, too."

Frank's eyes flickered. He said, "I think it's not like any case I've seen before."

Atkins cocked his head. "That," he said forcefully, "would be my threat assessment."

Frank watched a young girl avidly slake her thirst at the drinking fountain. He realized something. Mike *had* come to San Francisco to reassure him, of course. For that Frank felt grateful. But it wasn't the only reason Atkins was here. He also was on a mission to conserve the Millennium Group's resources. Namely, Frank Black. Atkins was concerned about losing Frank. Losing him to the emotional paralysis and near-lunacy that the first Polaroid mailing had inflicted, very nearly finishing Frank for good. The little girl at the water stand continued to gulp, with an eager simplicity that told Frank why he couldn't permit a return of the helplessness, the bleakness of three years before. There was a whole world that needed protection—a whole way of life in jeopardy that dwarfed his family's tiny microcosm, tiny plight.

Atkins had come here to remind Frank of this. Frank felt doubly grateful for it. "Thanks, Mike," he said.

Atkins shrugged. He said, "Tell me about what you've learned, Frank. Penseyres filled me in on the details as he understands them. But I want your perspective."

Frank took a deep breath. Then he described to Atkins much of what he'd seen so far.

Frank had lunch with Peter Watts at a Thai place two blocks from the Hall of Justice. They'd left word with the PD about their whereabouts in case of developments. Jim Penseyres meantime was working contacts with the San Francisco–area Russian expatriate community. As for Mike Atkins, he had declined to join Frank and Watts for lunch, citing Millennium Group business independent of the Auburn Park case.

Watts said over hot and sour shrimp soup, "You have any idea what Mike's working on?"

"He didn't mention it," Frank replied. "I didn't ask."

For a minute they consumed soup in silence.

Watts then said, "Frank, what do you think about requesting a PD stakeout at Acme Dry Cleaning? See if they can catch our dentist in action?"

"I'd say that's a good idea," Frank said, "if this were a more straightforward set of circumstances. But it's not. I have a feeling the dentist is wily. That he'd detect the stakeout, avoid it." Frank swallowed the last of his soup and attacked the sole remaining shrimp. "But you have a point. He might use Acme again. Something to keep in mind."

"Any ideas about that?" Watts asked.

Frank shook his head. "Not yet. We have so little to go on, Peter. We really do need a break."

Watts caught sight of Penseyres entering the restaurant and making a beeline for them. He said, "Maybe we got it."

Penseyres didn't take a seat. Nor did he say anything. Instead, he tossed a laminated ID card on the table.

Frank picked up the card and stared. Petaluma State College ID, with a color photo of a slightly sullen-looking young man. Frank frowned, deepening the grooves that bisected his cheeks. "That's him," he muttered. "The burn victim."

Under his breath Penseyres said exultantly, "*Yes.*"

"Eedo Bolow," Frank said, reading the printed name. To Watts he said, "Sounds Russian, Peter. I think we have a match."

Watts put his soup spoon down. "You got more?" he asked Penseyres.

Penseyres nodded. Watts waved for the waiter.

Lunch was over.

MILLENNIUM

CHAPTER

10

The rental car zipped through midday traffic. Watts drove. Frank rode shotgun, studying the contents of a folder—police forms and handwritten statements, a variety of paperwork. Penscyres occupied the rear. From it he said, "The dental records matched a missing persons report six months ago. The kid's parents filed it."

"Mother and father are naturalized citizens," Frank noted, studying a background sheet. "Immigrated from Chechnya in 1990 when the son was fifteen. Kid had a nice rap sheet. B and

E, minor assault, possession. Parents' address is 13235 Liberty Avenue."

Watts said sardonically, "Give me liberty or give me death."

Frank turned to Penseyres and asked, "Have the parents been notified?"

Penseyres nodded. "PD has officers there now," he said.

Eleven minutes later on Liberty Avenue, Watts pulled to the curb behind two black and white police cars. Across a small yard stood a modest Craftsman-style bungalow. The front door was open. A uniformed officer was waiting outside. Two others stood in the hall.

Frank, Watts, and Penseyres walked to the officer and exchanged brief greetings. Penseyres had something to discuss with the man. Frank and Watts went in the house.

The officers inside directed them to the dining room. There they found a heavyset fellow in his early fifties sitting at the table. He was dressed plainly but with care. His broad face radiated hurt, confusion, and deep suspicion.

"Mr. Bolow?" Frank said.

"Yes," said the man, his voice richly accented.

"I'm Frank Black. This is Peter Watts."

Mr. Bolow nodded without enthusiasm.

Frank said respectfully, "We're very sorry about your son."

Mr. Bolow didn't give an inch.

Watts said, "We're trying to find out how this might have happened to him."

Bolow said with mournful incredulity, "Six months you couldn't find Eedo, now you want me to help you?"

"We're not with the police, Mr. Bolow," Frank said in a tone both gentle and grave. A tone that rarely failed to elicit a response. "We believe your son might be one of several victims."

Bolow sighed explosively, as if suppressing a curse. Or tears. "He wouldn't listen to us," he said with sad anger. "Eedo had his own ideas. Put in his head by those friends of his."

Watts asked, "What friends, Mr. Bolow?"

"Driving all those German cars," Bolow replied, distaste coloring his voice. "All he could talk about, the cars. Then one day, Eedo comes home driving one, too."

"Do you know where he worked?" Frank asked.

"He said he couldn't tell us," Bolow snapped. "He said he was going to be *rich*." The man glared at Frank, disconsolate, bitter. "This is why we came to America?"

Watts cleared his throat and inquired, "Had you heard from him recently?"

Bolow stared at nothing for a moment. Reluctantly he said, "Six months ago he sent us a letter. A terrible letter. That's when we called the police." He stood, hands on the chair's arms for support, his fingers whitening. "My wife," he went on, casting an apprehensive glance down a hallway, "she wanted to burn it, she was so ashamed."

Bolow moved unsteadily down the hall. Someone stood beyond a doorway just out of Frank's view. The wife, Frank was sure. Bolow exchanged whispers with her. An anguished face poked from the doorway, conveying distrustful curiosity to Frank and Watts, mingled with despair. More whispers ensued. Twenty seconds passed. Then Mrs. Bolow thrust something at her husband.

Bolow lumbered back to Frank and Watts, holding an envelope. From it he took a one-page letter, which he handed to Frank. "It's in Russian," he said. "If you want me to translate . . ."

Frank said, "We wouldn't want to put you through that right now. But thank you for letting us read it."

"Mr. Bolow," Watts said. "It would be a big help if we could have a look at the envelope, too."

Bolow blinked, as if perplexed. He gave Watts the envelope. "Thank you, sir," Watts said.

"Thanks very much," Frank said. "We extend our sympathies to your wife."

An hour later in a darkened conference room off the PD forensics lab, Peter Watts turned on an overhead projector. Eedo Bolow's letter, written in Russian in an awkward scrawl, was emblazoned on a wallscreen. Watts approached the image and consulted notes he'd made. Then he turned to address Frank and Mike Atkins. They occupied chairs facing the screen, their attitude expectant.

"The salutation is to his mother," Watts explained. "He is disowning her, cutting the ties that prevent his ascendance to a higher stage." Watts paused, giving emphasis to what came next. "He says his birthrights and all his former worldly possessions have been burned in a sacrificial fire of his new faith."

Atkins said crisply, "Cult indoctrination."

Watts nodded. "There's a reference," he continued, "to fidelity and duty. And to burning in the fires of Gehenna if he should dishonor himself or his new brothers."

Frank stirred in his chair. "Gehenna?" he asked.

"Hebrew for hell," Atkins said.

Watts pressed on. "He says he's seen the All Powerful One in the pouring red rain and fears nothing but his wrath and vengeance."

Frank thought about the waterfall at Acme Dry Cleaning. Its patter into reddish puddles . . .

The lunging snout, the fangs, gnashing at Eedo Bolow's bloodied face . . .

"The end is coming," Watts further translated. "The numbers have been miscalculated. It says twenty-four times fifteen is three hundred and sixty. Adjustable by . . ."

"Two hundred and eighty-six point one," Atkins interrupted.

Frank and Watts stared at Atkins with suprise. The white-haired man took a deep breath and exhaled slowly. He said in a tone of quiet scorn, "There's a deliberate error in the Great Pyramid of Gizeh. An architectural anomaly that some prophets have cited as an error in our calculation of the true calendar year." Atkins smiled grimly. "Some people believe it sets the date of the Apocalypse in 1998."

From the door Penseyres interjected, "Plan your investment strategy accordingly."

Watts resumed the translation: "He says the weak and the indolent will perish. That he is with his new family now and must renounce his parents as he renounces his belief in anything but the power of the enterprise." Watts turned off the projector. In the sudden dimness he said with finality, "And the power of the enterprise resides in the hearts of the faithful."

"And," Frank added, "in the ashes of the dead."

Penseyres flipped a wall switch. The room brightened.

"Somebody really got into this kid's head," Watts declared.

Atkins shifted his chair to get a more direct view of Frank. "I'm not sure he's writing out of real faith," he commented.

Frank said, "I think he's writing out of fear."

"He could have been forced to write it," Watts pointed out.

Atkins shook his head. "Too many intransitive verbs."

"The imagery," Frank murmured. "It's very powerful. Very personal."

Atkins said with a pensive frown, "The use of the word Gehenna is strange. Its usage is archaic and only found in certain Old Testament translations." He gazed at Frank.

And added, "Somebody powerful got a hold on this kid. That's for sure."

"Or some*thing*," Frank said, his eyes hooded.

The others exchanged wary glances.

"Want to elaborate?" Watts said.

Frank said evasively, "We're dealing with a cult. Group psychology, manipulation, indoctrination. Vulnerable people separated from their families, backgrounds, pasts. It's not just one person who took hold of Eedo Bolow. It's an organization."

"Cults always have a supreme leader," Penseyres said. He gestured at Eedo Bolow's letter. "A Jim Jones, a David Koresh. The kid made a reference to 'the All Powerful One.'"

"'In the pouring red rain,'" Watts added. "That ring a bell, Frank?"

Frank nodded. It certainly did. He sent Mike Atkins a quick glance and said, "I can't speculate about the leader. But I wouldn't be surprised if the cult requires some uniformity of appearance from its members—short hair, for example. And I think we have to be prepared for the possibility that the organization has considerable resources at its disposal."

"What are you hinting at?" Watts asked.

Frank shook his head. He would speculate no further than what he'd already said.

D ylan scarcely listened to the P.M. education session. At lunch he'd overheard Ralph mention to Lars that he was considering a night on the town tonight. To Dylan that meant one of two things. Either Ralph really did intend to go out somewhere and blow off steam. Or someone had been scheduled for termination.

An acid-fueled rendezvous with the All Powerful, that is. At the abandoned factory down by the piers.

Dylan suspected the latter scenario.

Nights on the town were infrequent, carefully regulated events. Yet Ralph and Lars had gone bowling only a few nights before. On the same night that Dylan had helped dispose of Eedo's imperfectly powdered body, as a matter of fact. Furthermore, Ralph had sounded vague about his plans. Alarmingly so. A little too vague for him to have followed permission procedure.

Thus the chief question in Dylan's mind was: Who is it? Who's been chosen to die tonight?

It was possible that Ralph himself didn't know. Of the many mysteries shrouding the Enterprise's operation, decision making about termination ranked as one of the most secret, and unpredictable. Most of the guys didn't know a lot about it. Eedo, for example. Like all post-probation recruits, he'd seen the red rain, the face of the All Powerful. But prior to termination, he hadn't experienced the reality of what those things meant. He'd never been to the ruined factory, never had seen *its* falling water. Nor had he seen the highest honor of all, which doubled as the highest horror—the true face. The All Powerful unmasked.

Eedo hadn't even learned the symbolic importance of getting acid at Auburn Park.

The chump. He'd gone to his fate almost completely unaware.

Only the most favored and trusted were initiated to such matters. Technically, Dylan belonged to that elite. He'd participated in four terminations, for crying out loud. But now he had to wonder: Am I next?

Hence his inattention to the lecture. Dylan spent the entire hour focused on one subject: the hope that Ralph wouldn't invite him to go for a ride tonight.

His focus stayed with him in the shower room after the lecture. The dozens of loud sprays, the yells of pepped-up guys echoing off the tiles, the general pandemonium of water and soap and steam, seemed of another world. In response to Nick's enthusiasm about "hierarchies of slaves, a whole *caste system*," Dylan vacantly grinned. At Lars's heartfelt longing for "hummers that fucking *hover*, man," his eyes widened with awe not present. From Ralph he kept as far away as possible. He wished the steam would thicken. That he could evaporate into it.

Then came the boiler room session.

Dylan dressed for it rapidly, trying to psych himself up. Clean clothes, clean skin, clean mind—he'd shine today. He would make things happen.

With the others he filed into the boiler room, a large cement-walled space that contained eighty-odd work stations. They consisted of neatly aligned tables, three chairs to a table. Before each chair lay a pad of paper, freshly sharpened pencils, and a telephone. All the chairs faced in the same direction, toward the room's front.

Overhead, three mirror-surfaced hemispheres gleamed, mounted at intervals in the ceiling down the length of the room. Eyes-in-the-sky. Video surveillance pods.

At the head of the room stood a large videoscreen. On it blazed two words:

CREATE DESIRE

And it's just what I'll do, Dylan told himself as he slid behind his station. For the good of the Enterprise, I will *create desire*.

The room rustled with the readying of pencils and order pads. Ralph stood up front by the videoscreen, eyes glued to a wall clock. As the second hand swept to five seconds of three o'clock sharp, he inhaled deeply. When the second hand hit twelve, he barked, "In session!"

Six dozen young hands picked up telephone headpieces and put them to six dozen young ears. Six dozen fingers mashed automatic-dial buttons, placing computer-orchestrated calls to a preselected pool of numbers. The calls took varying amounts of time to connect. This varied the timing of a soft barrage of words that trained voices directed into dozens of telephone receivers, creating disjunctions in the mass repetition of mantralike pitch:

"Hi, my name is Bob Smith. I hope you have a moment, because I have a one-time offer on a new hair care product that I think you won't want to pass up. Would you like to try our product absolutely free? Terrific. I just need your name and address. Oh, and a credit card number for future purchases . . ."

Dylan settled into his "Bob Smith" persona, confident he'd unload tons of shampoo and conditioner. A whole truckful probably. Words flowed smoothly from his mouth, without a trace of the hesitation and dispiritedness that had plagued him yesterday. No, today's session would go just great. Dylan didn't doubt that at all. He would fill up lots and lots of order forms with neatly penciled information. With neatly penciled *numbers*.

He glanced at the nearest eye-in-the-sky, his sales pitch not faltering. The camera would record a damn fine performance at Station 64, that was for sure.

A new legend flashed onscreen:

EVERYBODY WANTS BEAUTIFUL HAIR

Three hours into the boiler room session, the wall clock hitting six o'clock, Dylan didn't feel entirely on track. He'd filled a few orders. Not enough to keep him on great terms with Ralph, however. Nor enough to impress the shiny hemispheres overhead. For some reason, the people answering his calls just weren't biting. Why?

Dylan wondered if he'd exaggerated his sense of competence earlier, at the start of the shift. Had he somehow tricked himself into thinking he was pitching smoothly?

He pressed the button for another automatic call. *Ring. Ring. Ring.* At the station next to Dylan, Lars brayed confidently into his phone, "Hi, my name is Bob Smith. I hope you have a moment, because I have a one-time offer on a new hair care product that I think. . . ."

Dylan glowered at Lars's smooth baby face. At eyes that knew no worry. At the mouth that worked the numbers. At the hand scribbling down numbers.

Suddenly, someone loomed. And said, "No new orders written?"

Dylan looked up. It was Ralph. Of course. To him Dylan muttered, "Not yet."

Ralph gazed down, his expression blank but damning.

Dylan stared back, feeling his own face wilt. As if his features were melting. Decomposing. Burning.

Ralph moved along.

He didn't even say anything, Dylan thought. He just *looked at me.* "Terrific," Nick was saying two stations to Dylan's right. "All I need is your name and address. Oh, and a credit card number for future purchases."

Dylan became aware of the fact that the number he had called no longer was ringing. That someone had answered, in fact. A querulous voice was saying, "Hellooww? Is anybody *there?*"

Dylan mumbled, "Hi, my name is Bob Smith. I hope you have a moment. . . ."

Dusk was falling when Catherine pulled her minivan into the Black residence's driveway. The new security light, sensing the van's rolling bulk, ignited.

Catherine got out and walked around to the passenger-side door. Jordan, inside, was sleeping. "Wake up, sweetie," Catherine said as she opened the door. "We're home."

Jordan stirred, but didn't wake. Catherine picked her up and closed the car door. She carried her daughter to the house's rear entrance, and then inside.

Across the street, a man sitting in a parked car watched lights go on in ground-floor rooms. And then, in a second-floor room as well.

Minutes later Bennie was watching Catherine put Jordan in bed. Since Jordan clearly wasn't disposed to play tonight—she still was sound asleep—Bennie decided to go downstairs.

His destination was his water bowl in the kitchen. But instead of making the left turn there, he paused in the front hall.

Moments later Catherine came down the stairs. She saw Bennie standing stock-still in the hall. "Are you waiting for me?" she asked.

Bennie didn't move. Catherine noticed that his attention was focused on the front door; she stooped down to pick up mail and said, "Do you want to go outside?"

Bennie continued to stare at the door, at its expanse of dark glass.

Catherine glanced at the door.

Outside, pressed to the glass, stood a dark silhouette. The outlines of a hefty, silent man. A man staring directly at her.

Catherine clapped a hand to her mouth, letting loose a muffled gasp of fright.

MILLENNIUM
CHAPTER

12

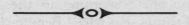

Catherine stood rooted to the floor, her heart pounding a staccato machine-gun rhythm, her mind leaping beyond her front door to the threats that she'd spent years trying to ward off. All the menace she and Frank had confronted together over the years—the stalker, the Polaroids, the anonymous terror campaign—suddenly condensed into that looming silhouette.

A realization chilled her. Who in the vicinity might help? Whom did she know? Jack Meredith? Not the most reassuring of backups, Jack. *I'm completely alone*, Catherine thought. *With Jordon.*

Slowly she stepped backward, running a mental review of items she could use for defense. The umbrella in the corner? No, not heavy enough. Something in the kitchen? Plenty of things, but what? Bennie? Forget it, his tail was wagging. The phone—she'd call 911, pray that people got here before the man broke in. . . .

Behind the door a voice rumbled, "Catherine?"

Again she froze. For several seconds she stood still, unable to reply.

The man tapped the door and said, "Catherine, it's Bob Bletcher."

Catherine exhaled raggedly. She took a few tentative steps toward the door. "Bob?" she quavered.

"Yeah."

Menace drained from the dark silhouette. Catherine went to the door, a hand reaching down to get a grip on Bennie's collar. Part of her remained in emergency mode; that part saw a need to restrain the puppy, just in case he made a lunge for Bob's throat. She opened the door.

Lieutenant Bob Bletcher of the Seattle Police Department stood stolidly on the

porch, dressed in civilian clothes. "Is everything okay?" he inquired, concern tinging his
voice.

"Yeah," Catherine replied with something
of a gasp. She gazed at Bletcher's gruff, no-
nonsense, and entirely unthreatening face.
"Actually," she confessed, "you scared me half
to death."

Bletcher blinked at her. "I'm sorry," he
said in sincerely apologetic tones. "I was . . ."
Hesitation clouded his eyes, suggesting that
he hadn't expected a need to explain himself,
and now was groping for a tactful way to do
it. "Frank gave me a call asking if I could stop
by," he said. "I think he was a little worried
about you and Jordan."

Catherine absorbed Bletcher's comments.
"Oh God," she blurted. "Bob—*I'm* sorry.
Thank you! We're fine, actually."

"You're sure?" Bletcher asked, his voice
doubtful.

Catherine nodded. "I just wasn't expecting anyone," she went on, embarrassed she'd
reacted in a manner so off the mark. She gave
Bletcher a wan grin. "Would you like to come
in, Bob?"

"No, no," he said briskly. "I know you've
got your little girl to put to bed—"

"Hold it," Catherine interrupted, with a

firmness that would brook no dissent. "I'm going to make some coffee. Okay?"

Bletcher shrugged, resigning himself to the inevitable. Catherine clearly would have her way. "Okay," he said, reaching down to give the avid Bennie a pat on the head.

Dylan stood in the Enterprise cafeteria line, feeling no hunger but trying, as best he could, to keep up a front. He was just one of the guys. Tired, like the rest, after another whack at the numbers. To look at him you couldn't tell he wasn't craving whatever nourishment the institutional caterers had delivered this evening—chicken pot pie or turkey sausages or gray London broil, the usual fare accompanied by mounds of pasta, mashed potatoes. Yes, Dylan looked normal. As if he were anticipating not just dinner but a little relaxation thereafter—instructional videos, the free hour from nine to ten. And then, of course, hitting his bunk. Sleep. Dreamless sleep.

But Dylan didn't look forward to any of those things. He knew the pitfalls now. Not even sleep was safe. Nothing was, after

today's pitiful performance in the boiler
room. He stood in line praying that Ralph
wouldn't come over and tell him—casually?
Or not so casually?—that a little ride was in
the cards tonight.

Someone tapped Dylan on his shoulder.
Dylan turned. Ralph stood there, staring at
him blankly. Unreadably.

Dylan did his best to control a shiver.

"We need to talk," Ralph said, putting a
hand on Dylan's elbow. Dylan stumbled a bit
as Ralph guided him away from the food line.
Together they walked clear across the cafeteria to an exit to one of the stairwells. Dylan
passed through the door, conscious of puzzled
eyes following their progress. Wondering
what could be going on.

The metal door swung shut, the hiss of its
pneumatic push whooshing through the stairwell's chilly, concrete-walled air. With a sharp
clank that echoed down to the basement and
up to the bunkroom on the second floor, the
door sealed Dylan and Ralph into as private a
space as could be found at this hour. All the
other squadmates were in the mess.

Not eating with Dylan and Ralph, appar-
ently. Dylan couldn't tell what the hell was
up. Whatever it was, it had to be terrible.
Dylan knew of no precedent for this kind of

ad hoc meeting. Even terminations didn't disrupt routine. . . .

Then Dylan understood.

Of course, he was about to be terminated. And of course, the termination wouldn't follow procedure. Why? Because Dylan was privy to the procedure. He'd helped carry it out on four separate occasions. Unlike Eedo and the others, a nighttime visit to Auburn Park wouldn't mystify him. Nor would the acid, nor the abandonment ritual at the ruined factory. Dylan was familiar with every last step of the process. Which meant, obviously, that a different process was called for. It's simple, Dylan concluded. The Leader had told Ralph to get rid of him by some other means.

Maybe right here in the stairwell.

Ralph put a hand on Dylan's chest and pushed. Dylan didn't resist; he staggered backward until he hit a wall. The hand continued to press. Dylan's back flattened against the wall, his legs and arms did as well, his open palms, too—Ralph had him spread-eagled against cold concrete.

The hand stopped pressing. Ralph put his own hands to the wall, on either side of Dylan's head. He leaned in close, closer, until their noses were almost touching. His eyes held a gleam; he said, "We have a problem."

Dylan almost nodded. He didn't because he would have touched Ralph's head.

The gleaming eyes bored into Dylan's eyes. The corners of the mouth turned up: a mirthless smile. The mouth said, "How do we terminate a brother who has terminated others?"

Dylan started blinking and couldn't stop. Ralph's face blurred. Everything blurred; Dylan thought he'd pass out.

"I'll tell you how we do it," Ralph whispered. "We deceive him. We inform him that someone else requires termination. And that he, the real terminee, will participate."

Oh, thought Dylan. *Why is he explaining this? To me?*

"Tonight," whispered Ralph. "Tonight we're performing a termination. You're on the team, Dylan. Any objections?"

Curiosity, and a strange clarity, spread through Dylan's mind. Although he knew the answer perfectly well, he asked, "Who is the terminee?"

Ralph's mouth widened with a leer. The mouth said, "You think it's you, don't you?"

Dylan stared at Ralph's teeth. Perfect teeth. Improved, probably, with orthodontics.

"It's not you. It's Nick."

"Nick?" Dylan muttered.

"Yeah. Our buddy who keeps reliving a jazz concert, over and over. Or didn't you notice?"

"I noticed," Dylan whispered. "Thought it was strange."

"Yeah. Well. Strange doesn't bother the Leader. But crazy does. We don't need crazies here, do we, Dylan?"

"No, Ralph. Sure don't."

"You're not crazy, Dylan. Right?"

"No way," Dylan said faintly.

"Of course not." Ralph detached his right hand from the wall and pinched Dylan's cheek. Dylan winced; Ralph's eyes bored harder. "We'll leave at nine-thirty. Two cars. But me, you, Lars, and Nick in the same car—like the night we did Eedo."

"Okay," Dylan said, his head swimming. "Uh—who does Nick think is going to get it?"

Ralph chuckled. "Why, that would be you, Dylan. Nick thinks the Leader wants you."

Catherine deposited herself on a chair at her dining room table, careful to keep steady her freshly brewed cup of coffee. Bob Bletcher occupied another chair at the table, savoring the steam rising from his own cup, its aroma enriched with cream and four spoonfuls of sugar. Although both he and Catherine had an inkling of what they soon would discuss, neither quite knew how to start the conversation. Twenty seconds passed as they took their first sips of the beverage that guaranteed a certain alertness, at least. Catherine had put Jordan in bed—a swift process tonight, since the child had been sound asleep in the minivan.

There was little chance that Jordan would overhear things she shouldn't.

Finally Catherine said, "How much has he told you?"

Bletcher studied his cup. "About his breakdown?" he asked.

Catherine nodded.

"Only a little more than I'd already heard," Bletcher said slowly. "He mentioned the numbing that comes with the territory. How the cruelty, the unspeakable crimes, become depersonalized—after a while, he said, you stop feeling it. You block it out. A kind of mental novocaine kicks in." Bletcher glanced at Catherine. Looking for permission to go on.

Catherine met his eyes tranquilly.

"Then he told me about the Polaroids that someone took of you and Jordan," Bletcher continued. "Sent to him anonymously, a year after he'd cracked a particularly gruesome case—which involved a serial killer who would butcher entire households at random, then send Polaroids of the victims to the police. So when Frank got the anonymous Polaroids of you, he saw it as a threat. And suddenly he couldn't leave the house. The mental novocaine wore off. He was afraid to leave you alone."

"He was paralyzed, Bob," Catherine said earnestly. "Not just by fear, though. By something much deeper. By understanding."

Bletcher examined his rough-hewn hands. "He talked about that too," he said, choosing his words with care. "About being able to see into the darkness. That he'd developed a kind of facility to see what a killer sees."

Catherine settled back in her chair. She said quietly, "As well as you know him, Bob. As long as you worked together . . . I don't think anyone can appreciate exactly what that must be like."

"No," Bletcher said simply. He smiled and added, "But I'm sure you know better than anyone."

Catherine returned the smile thinly. "It's

interesting," she remarked. "In my work I deal with so many troubled people. Victims, mostly. The kind of work I do, the clinical therapy—I have such an opportunity to change and affect people's lives. But Frank can't do that."

Bletcher raised his eyebrows. "I don't know if I understand," he said. "What do you mean?"

"Most of us," Catherine replied, "work with a certain amount of optimism that we can make a difference. Sometimes I think of Frank as the Catcher in the Rye, standing at the edge of the cliff and trying to save the world. But he can't change anything. All he can do is catch these horrible men before they kill again."

Bletcher murmured, "Frank told me it was his gift. And his curse.."

Catherine nodded. "I didn't understand at first how he did it. How he ever went back to work."

Bletcher sat forward a bit, lifted his hand casually. A little too casually; he didn't know how to conceal his ongoing fascination with the exact nature of Frank's work. Nor was he sure he should pump Catherine for info on it. He said in his most noncommittal voice, "He was approached by this—Millennium Group."

"Yes," said Catherine. "But Frank went

back because he had to. It's who he is. And that's why I can never let him think that Jordan and I aren't perfectly safe in this perfect house and perfect world he's tried to give us. Because if he ever thought differently, I know next time he'd never be able to leave."

Bletcher gazed at Catherine, wishing he could come up with a comforting way to disagree. But he couldn't. And he could tell from Catherine's steady eyes that she knew he knew he couldn't.

Catherine smiled at him. "Thanks, Bob," she said. "It's nice of you to stop by. Above and beyond—I really appreciate it."

MILLENNIUM
CHAPTER

13

The two BMWs sped from the Haight past Golden Gate Park.

Industrial frat-rock music throbbed in the lead car, the bass lines thundering through the windows, the seats, the floor, through four young men with close-cropped hair. Lars drove. Ralph rode shotgun.

Dylan and Nick sat in the rear. The music's volume made conversation difficult, which was just as well from the points of view of both Dylan and Nick. Neither wanted to talk. Particularly with each other.

Dylan had done quite a bit of thinking about the purpose of tonight's mission. Through his abbreviated attendance at dinner, through the video period that followed, and through the free hour after that—like dinner, cut short—he'd wrestled with the possibility that in actual fact it was he, not Nick, who would burn tonight.

Why should he believe what Ralph had said? Could Ralph have fingered Nick because Dylan knew what a termination entailed? And might try to resist it? In other words, was the talk in the stairwell just a ploy to lull Dylan into a false sense of security?

Maybe. Dylan couldn't deny, though, that the guy sitting next to him *was* a little crazy. Nick's persistent retelling of the jazz concert experience did smack of loose screws. But then, in Dylan's opinion, none of his Enterprise brothers could claim certifiable sanity. This opinion had taken shape only recently to be sure, during a time of unusual stress—amid circumstances that Dylan knew full well might have affected his own judgment. He'd even suspected himself of being nuts. At times he'd been *sure* of it.

Nonetheless, he'd had to wonder about Ralph's claim that the Leader could deal with "strange" but not with "crazy." If Nick really

were crazy, so crazy he had to be killed, then
to Dylan it seemed logical that most of his
barracks-mates deserved death. Including, of
course, himself. Especially himself.

And Ralph knew this. He knew that the
logic applied just as well to Dylan as to
Nick. Obviously he did, he'd seen Dylan
behave oddly, do things like sleep through
reveille. So yeah, Ralph had grounds for
considering Dylan nuts. And of course
Ralph knew that *Dylan* knew this. So what
was Ralph doing, mind torture? Creating
horrible suspense? Sharpening punishment
in advance?

Maybe the Leader had told him to set up
both Dylan and Nick.

Then again, Nick appeared nervous.

Which had been giving Dylan hope.

The headlights behind them flared in the
rearview mirror, sending a wash of light
across Nick's face. He stared fixedly ahead,
his eyes on the road but his thoughts elsewhere; or so it seemed to Dylan, who had
watched Nick become progressively more
absentminded tonight.

At dinner, after the stairwell conversation
with Ralph, Dylan had studied Nick closely,
looking for signs of jitters. Signs of fear. He'd
wanted to know if Nick was entertaining the

same set of possibilities that he had conceived: Who's really going to get it? Me? Or him?

Twice, Nick met Dylan's gaze. The first time, Nick quickly looked away, his complexion coloring a bit, as if with shame—as if he'd been caught doing something vile. Such as thinking, for example, about the fact that later tonight he would help send someone to hell. That didn't reassure Dylan. He knew the feeling; he'd experienced it himself on four different occasions, most keenly during the latest one, when he had watched Eedo, clueless Eedo, consume his final meal. That hadn't been a barrel of laughs. Dylan actually had felt pretty ill. So no, the reddening complexion hadn't done Dylan any good at all.

But then came the second time he and Nick locked eyes. Nick was bringing a spoonful of mashed potatoes to his mouth. A heaping spoonful, quivery, gravy-greased. A split second before its delivery, two inches from the mouth, Nick must have felt the stare again, for the spoon froze midair, and Nick's eyes flicked, with the mechanical swivel of a doll's eyes, directly at Dylan. But this time, Nick held the gaze. And his face didn't flush; it paled. It went white as a sheet, as if the mind behind it felt sudden, major dread. And for several long seconds he didn't look away. He seemed paralyzed in fact. As if terror had seized him—a deer, transfixed by oncoming high-beams.

When Dylan saw this, he thought: Nick's looking at death.

And it was Dylan's turn to blush. His face went hot; it grew hotter as he watched the quivery glop of mashed potato slide off Nick's spoon and fall on his lap, Nick's eyes meanwhile staying frozen in place, showing no awareness of spilled food, showing only the stark fear of one who knows he's doomed.

Dylan broke the eye contact and didn't look at Nick again during the rest of dinner.

But he did look during the videos. And during the thirty minutes of free hour before Ralph ordered them, along with Lars and five other guys who'd never participated in a termination before, to assemble in the garage. Dylan didn't make eye contact again, he now lacked the stomach. He just wanted more evidence for something he desperately needed to believe—that Nick feared for his life.

Dylan did see more evidence. Nick gradually zombified. He seemed to lose connection with the here and now, to scarcely be aware of anything around him.

Dead man walking? Dylan hoped so. Nothing personal, of course. He didn't hate Nick. Not at all.

But he also didn't want to play victim tonight. And if Nick had reasons to think that he, Nick, would fill that role, then Dylan could believe just a bit more easily the veracity of what Ralph had said.

Who knew? Maybe Nick had screwed up in ways that Dylan hadn't even heard about.

Dylan fervently hoped so. The car pulled to the curb, and the second BMW pulled up behind, rousing him from his meditations. Through his window he surveyed a dark stretch of road. Trees, shrubs, a sign marking a dimly lit path:

AUBURN MEMORIAL PARK AND GARDENS.

The place looked different tonight. Dylan and his companions craned necks to get views deeper in. The park's central area, beyond a dense screen of trees, was glowing. The rose garden lay in that area; for some reason, bright lights burned there. A public event? A festival? Some kind of police action?

At night? Dylan couldn't recall any such event at Auburn Park. Didn't mean they didn't happen, though.

"Weird," Lars remarked.

Ralph stared at the glow, his lips compressed with irritation. "Don't think it's a problem," he muttered. "Nick. Dylan. You two and Kevin were the last ones here. Remember?"

Nick and Dylan nodded.

"Either of you see anything funny?"

"No," Nick said too quickly.

Ralph turned to face Nick, his movement a forceful lurch, his suede jacket squeaking against his seat's leather upholstery. "You sure about that?" Ralph demanded.

Nick nodded with vigor.

Ralph stared at Dylan. "You?" he asked.

Dylan had indeed seen something funny the last time he'd been here. But he didn't think it advisable to inform Ralph of that. He shrugged and said as casually as he could, "Everything was normal. No lights. Just me, Nick, and Kevin. And the usual scumbags drifting through."

Ralph got out of the car and strode down the path.

Dylan watched him disappear, praying that the lights in the rose garden were, in fact, a problem. A police sweep, for example. A public safety campaign. A massive effort to drive drug dealers from the park.

The idea fascinated Dylan. No acid to jump-start the termination? Unheard of.

Acid was what made terminations so much fun.

So maybe Ralph would call it off. Dylan glanced to his left. Nick was clasping his hands between his knees. Dylan saw why. Slightly, but perceptibly, Nick was trembling.

The poor guy, thought Dylan, feeling both a jolt of empathy and sudden relief. Nick was looking more and more like tonight's main event.

Nick should run, Dylan found himself thinking. Just open his door, get out, and run. Dylan wondered if he should try to tell Nick that. The same thing he'd told Eedo Bolow outside Acme Dry Cleaning.

But Dylan had a problem with giving such advice—he himself wouldn't follow it. Even if he were one hundred percent sure he faced death.

He recalled the various times he'd considered escape. He'd concluded each time he wouldn't succeed. Couldn't succeed.

There was no escape. Not from Gehenna.

―◉―

Ralph walked through the park with a mounting sense of disbelief. The place was a mob scene, full of milling people who had no business being here. Mobile klieg lights rendered it almost day-bright. Cops had cordoned it off. TV cameras pointed at it, as did numerous impassioned fingers.

Snatches of talk among passersby soon gave Ralph a clue to what was going on:

"No question they're human. . . ."

"Dump trucks, I heard. . . ."

"Did you hear about the leg?"

"Nobody knows, but some people are saying dozens and dozens. Burned to ashes . . ."

Ralph didn't need to hear much more than that. He wheeled away, heading to the spot where he often found what he wanted.

The old hippie sat on his regular bench, behind a bank of flowering rhododendrons. The half-full moon and the filtered rose garden kliegs put a silverish glaze on his wrinkles, his pale ponytail, his ratty embroidered shoulder bag. Ralph waited for him to finish a transaction with three feral-looking teens and then took a seat on the bench.

"Busy tonight," he remarked.

The hippie nodded in agreement. "The usual?" he inquired.

"Yeah," said Ralph.

From his shoulder bag the hippie extracted a small foil-wrapped packet. Ralph gave him a couple of twenties for it, then got up and asked idly, "Do they know who's messing with the garden?"

"Nope," replied the hippie with a smile.

"What exactly did they find?"

"Lot of stories," said the hippie reflectively. "The one I tend to believe concerns a wheelbarrow or two of carbonized human bone. Fine ash. Much finer than crematory-fine." His eyes flashed with amusement. "And an ear."

"What?" Ralph demanded.

"Burned around the edges, intact in the middle," the hippie murmured. "A human ear."

"Why?" Ralph said. "I mean—do they know?"

The old man shrugged. "Just another psychopath."

Dylan sat in the car wondering what was keeping Ralph, and what the hell was happening in the park. Lars had turned off the stereo to avoid attracting attention. The relative silence was bringing a bonus: audible comments of passersby. So far the voices hadn't yielded much of note. Dylan found himself listening with greater interest to the sound of Nick's shallow, rapid breathing.

A couple hurried from the park, a man and a woman, middle-aged, talking intently. As they passed the car the woman exclaimed, "Ghoulish as all get out!"

Lars turned his baby face to Dylan. "What's bothering her?" he said with innocent blandness. Then his eyebrows rose suggestively. Mock-ghoulishly.

Shithead, thought Dylan. He listened to Nick's breathing become shallower, quicker. Nick almost was panting.

"Ah," said Lars, now gazing at the path to the park. "Speaking of ghouls—the Dark Prince returns."

Dylan glimpsed Ralph trotting down the path. He got to the car, stuck his head through the passenger-side window, and glanced at Dylan and Nick.

"No go?" Lars asked him.

Ralph didn't reply immediately. The sight of Nick panting, of Dylan sitting stone-still, engrossed him. From a pocket he produced the foil packet. He handed it to Lars; continuing to eyeball the occupants of the back seat, he said grimly, "Tickets. To the show."

The horror show, Dylan thought with a mental twitch.

Lars unfolded the packet, examined the strip of perforated paper within, tore off five of the small postage-stamp-like squares, and, with a macabre flourish, deposited the squares in Ralph's waiting palm.

Ralph went to the BMW idling behind them, delivered the doses, and returned. He got in, slammed his door hard. Conversationally he said to Lars, "I just found out the most amazing thing."

"Yeah?" Lars said, giving Ralph the remaining acid.

"Yeah," replied Ralph, his casual tone staying steady. "The city's in an uproar because somebody made a grisly discovery in the rose garden. I wonder how that happened?"

Neither Nick nor Dylan had an answer to the question. Nick because he was baffled. Dylan because his throat was drying; so thoroughly, he lost faith in his ability to speak.

Lars asked, "You're talking ashes?"

"More than ashes," Ralph said thoughtfully, shifting his gaze to the parking brake between the front seats.

In Dylan's mind, bells were tolling.

A crowd of people streamed from the park, the babble of their voices indistinct but carrying the unmistakable tone of outrage. Ralph stared at them for a few seconds. Then he said, "Someone's been sloppy. I'll tell you one thing—the Leader won't be happy."

Dylan felt an unexpected stab of guilt. He realized he'd made a mistake. Yeah, the Leader now had a problem. Maybe a really big one. And it was Dylan's fault.

Ralph leaned in close to Lars's head and started whispering.

Dylan tried to make out what Ralph was saying. He couldn't really, Ralph's voice was too low. But once or twice, Dylan thought he heard the word "ear."

I shouldn't have left it there, Dylan thought with dull self-reproach. It was stupid to leave it there. Of course someone would find it. And of course that would cause an investigation. And of course the investigation would find the ashes. Which of course would cause a public outcry. Of course . . . Why hadn't he thought of that?

Why hadn't he simply put the ear in his pocket? And then dumped the thing in a sewer or something?

Then again, Dylan told himself, it wasn't my fault that the ear hadn't burned to ashes. Was it?

Ralph and Lars continued to whisper. Dylan wondered if they were cooking up a story that would make them innocent in the eyes of the Leader. Or if they were cooking up a story that would make Dylan look guilty— that seemed pretty likely. Especially considering that Dylan *was* guilty . . .

"Listen guys," Nick blurted at Ralph and Lars, "I don't know what this problem is. I really don't. And I *really* hope you're not going to pin it on *me*."

To Dylan, Nick's tone carried an alarming tang of sincerity.

Ralph gave Nick an impassive stare, then gave Dylan the same. Dylan started sweating. "Me too!" he declared, trying to echo Nick's conviction. Lamely he added, "Anyway. What *is* the problem?"

Ralph smiled. "Don't worry," he said with a quietness that sounded crafty, bordering on sinister. "Be happy." He studied the acid-laced squares in his hand.

"Hey," Nick said, his jaw muscles bunched. "The Leader sees through lies. Whatever this is, he'll know I didn't do it. He will. He'll know."

"That's right," Dylan agreed loudly. "The Leader will know it wasn't me. He'll find the guy." *I'm done for*, he thought with despair.

"Yeah," Ralph said. "Sure." He licked the tip of a finger, snared an acid dose with the fingertip, and extended it to Nick. "Fetch the paper," he said.

Nick shuddered. "Okay," he said. "Let's do it." He tweezered the hit with forefinger and thumb, then jammed it in his mouth. His eyes bright with defiance, he chewed.

Ralph's finger pushed a dose at Dylan.

"Cool," Dylan quavered.

"Take it," said Ralph.

"Yeah," said Dylan, his mind emptying into a cistern of blackness. "No problem, Ralph."

"Go ahead," said Ralph. "Take it."

"Sure," Dylan said. "I want three hits."

Ralph's eyebrows twitched.

"That's right," Dylan whispered. He had to prove himself, his fitness to belong.

"No problem," said Ralph, dabbing up more squares. "Knock yourself out."

MILLENNIUM
CHAPTER

15

Ten minutes later Dylan felt the acid ignite. His stomach burned, his body buzzed; his mind acquired a corrosive fizz. Never before had he taken this much at one time. Oh well. Why hold back now?

Why hold anything back? Dylan thought about fear. Frontiers of fear, places he soon would visit, but couldn't begin to imagine. He already felt more afraid than he ever had felt in his entire life; a pure state of mind, without defined boundaries, it promised much more to come. It was inescapable, too. So why fight this? Why not embrace it?

Why not heighten the fear? Take it as far as he could? In preparation for the certainty that the Leader would take it light-years beyond?

No real preparation existed for that, of course. But Dylan experienced a curious sensation just thinking about it—a kind of coldly incandescent thrill. Someone once had told him that the root meaning of the word *ecstasy* was "standing outside of oneself." Dylan never had understood that. Stand outside? Of oneself? What were the kicks there? Now he did understand, for although he faced ecstasy's opposite, its polar-negative charge, he indeed seemed outside. Not just of himself, however. He felt terminally out the door. Out of this level of existence, through the outermost exits to an enormity that made the car, Ralph, Lars driving, Nick shivering, and yes, himself— seem like special effects. Like a poor simulation. Dated, irrelevant, fake.

About to be turned off.

But interesting in its way. In its strange, funny way. Dylan felt a pang of nostalgia for life as he'd known it. Miserable though he'd lately been, sick at heart, his faith and discipline eroding, he'd still remained a fit young man of twenty-two. A guy who might have pulled himself together, gotten savvy, regained focus. Had things gone just a little better he might even have been cruising into a great future. Riches and glory. The solidarity of his brothers. All that.

Instead, what did he have? The back seat of a BMW he'd never ride again. Three former brothers who now loathed and feared him. A San Francisco night bearing the briny tang of a storm, dark skies that promised to water, somewhere, a bed for his ashes. All of it looking and feeling like a bad computer game—programmed to deliver dead meat called Dylan to a ruined factory building.

No wonder he felt outside. The acid, naturally, was enhancing the sensation. The fake car, the fake darkness smearing beyond the windows, the fake guys riding with his own fake body—a body that Dylan was coming to perceive as sitting *beside* him—all these things were seriously tingling around the edges. Not as if they were losing resolution, like a holodeck scene degrading. More as if the generative software were breaking through, fraying the surface, becoming visible, revealing the artifice *below the surface*—revealing the digital swarm that created this illusion.

In other words, revealing the numbers.

The numbers. Our empty essence, thought Dylan. It's what makes us and breaks us, it's all we are in life's big boiler room, and it's a whole lot of nothing. A fantasy that seems solid to the hungry and eager, but which is just a plaything, a huge, transparent toy, for the ultimate number cruncher. For the being who's got *all* the numbers. For the thing who soon will demonstrate that mine is up.

Then Dylan caught sight of something else.

Nick. Staring at Dylan. With great effort Dylan forced himself to say, "Trouble seeing me, Nick?"

The words came out incompletely, like a flawed transmission. Missing digits. Low res.

Nick said quietly, "I see you." His mouth twitched as he added, "You're dead."

"Dead," Dylan whispered. That didn't seem right. Fake, yes; dead, no. Outside, yes; gone, no. Evaporating, yes; a corpse, no.

Nick pointed at him and said more loudly, "Dead."

"I'm disappearing," Dylan informed the idiot.

Ralph turned around and regarded the fake occupants of the fake back seat. Headlight beams blazed through the windshield, wreathing his head with a fiery corona. It looked as if he'd acquired a fake crown of flames. . . . Ralph seemed to enjoy it, because he smiled.

Then he said, "Disappearing? You're not invisible, Dylan. But Nick's right. You *are* dead."

The crown of flames ebbed, faded, leaving an afterglow aura that imparted authority, even reality, to Ralph's staring face. In Dylan, in the teeming fizz that remained, something shuddered. A memory flashed through, replaying a comment that Lars earlier had made. A comment about Ralph, as a matter of fact. Lars had said, "Speaking of ghouls—the Dark Prince returns."

Ghoul, thought Dylan with sudden certitude. *That's what he is.* Ralph's face changed, bringing proof. It wizened, dried, went simian. The cheeks hollowed. The brow, lips, and jaw thickened. Shiny hairs coiled from the nostrils. The eyes lit with a dull, impenetrable glow.

"Dead," repeated the ghoul. It grinned, exposing blood-red fangs.

This didn't look fake to Dylan. The car still seemed fake; but Ralph the ghoul looked very real, and Dylan suddenly knew why. Ralph had traveled to the outside, too. Like Dylan, he'd passed into a new dimension. Which meant something terrible. Something really, really bad.

Dylan doubted he could make the ghoul go away.

He tore his eyes from it and looked at Lars. Lars wasn't driving. Another ghoul sat at the wheel—stained tusks, matted fur. Claws on the wheel. Reek of sulphur . . . Dylan turned to Nick. He wasn't there either. A third ghoul shared the back seat. Through clenched teeth, tiny and sharp, it hissed at Dylan.

Dylan couldn't look at that. Beyond the windows, the darkness sliding by remained fake, clearly not real. But the things in the car weren't fake at all. Dylan knew why. They were escorts with a mission—taking him to the bad place.

And they couldn't be stopped.

"Dead!" hissed the ghoul that used to be Nick.

The driving ghoul nodded. "Dead," it agreed.

The Ralph-ghoul, still staring, chortled. "Very dead," it declared.

Dylan raised an arm to fend off the stare. Even though his arm couldn't really fend . . .

It wasn't fizzing. His arm—it wasn't evaporating into the thin air.

Dylan beheld rotten flesh instead. Putrescent, flayed flesh, the bone below exposed. Slimy bone, glistening, pale. The rest of his body looked the same—his chest, his legs, his skeleton feet, everything a mass of horrid decay.

A *corpse*, thought Dylan. *I'm dead.*

The car took a sharp turn to the left. Dylan remembered this turn; it went to the bad place. He looked out and saw he was correct. A peeling sign, whitish against a building's dark hulk, bore words he knew well:

ACME DRY CLEANING

Dylan studied the sign. For some reason, it looked real.

Then the car, both cars actually, were going around and around—turning, turning, turning, the headlights streaking across industrial facades, seeming to revolve the facades around a pivot, revolve them around the hub of this dream, around its dead core—around the rotting flesh that once went by the name of Dylan.

The turn stopped. The two cars, facing each other across a ten-foot divide, exchanged high-beam glares.

From the roof of Acme's ruined plant—Through night vision goggles—Watching—Watching the

young men emerge from the cars—Watching
Ralph signal the five new ones, the initiates, those
who had followed—Watching those five—They
spill into the fire of headlights eye-to-eye—There
they form a nest—A snare—

A snare for Dylan—

Dylan exited the car feeling pretty mobile for
a corpse. It confused him, the open air, the
dark immensity above. The blazing pool of
headlights confused him as well. This wasn't
going according to expectations. It pleased
him for obscure reasons, reasons he couldn't
name, which he knew was stupid. But why
not be stupid?

Why not take stupidity to its farthest limits?

So he smiled. As stupidly as he could.

And saw the milling group of guys.

Young guys. New ones, Enterprise fresh-
men. Unlike Ralph, Lars, and Nick, they
didn't look ghoulish.

They looked demonic. Like young, hungry
demons. Worse than ghouls because, physi-
cally speaking, they appeared quite human—
normal, rugged boys with very short hair.

But they weren't what they seemed. Dylan

knew this. He knew it from their attitude.
These guys had the attitude of fiends from hell.
Freshman fiends, that is—candidate fiends—
Dylan knew that these were the worst of all.

He'd been one himself, once. A fiend getting in his very first licks.

A tall kid raised a hand, clawed it as if his
fingers were talons, and uttered a chilling,
crowlike sound: "*Caw!*"

Caw? thought Dylan, his vision blurring.

Then they all were doing it: "*Caw! Caw!*"

In Dylan's head, comprehension crept in,
with reminders of why he was here. He froze,
feeling the sting of raw terror. The *caws* were
puncturing his will like fangs striking skin;
injecting venom that stilled every muscle,
shriveled any shred of an instinct to flee, to
resist.

So he just stood there, taking it: "*Caw!
Caw!*"

Then suddenly the fiends and the ghouls
were piling into their respective cars. Doors
slammed; windows whirred down; bass lines
boomed through the dark factory-lined space.

Dylan stood alone in the bath of fire.

Tires squealed, the headlights rapidly
backed up; the cars started circling in tandem,
like wolves coordinating the torment, the
guys leaning out the windows, yelling, jeering.

Dylan quaked as he absorbed this next-to-last stage of his ordeal; his mind slid, drained, lost its wits. Headlights and taillights trailed luminous blurs, spinning a vortex that left him no choice—he was obliged to blunder into the final stage. Obliged to follow the ritual all the way through.

And he did. With the blind surrender of a man racing toward a cliff's edge, or leaping from a volcano's lip, he ran at Acme's crumbled front wall. Closer, closer came the shadowed hole, the vast gloom within. Terminal adrenaline propelled him, along with a weird exhilaration of terror—the perfect state of mind for plunging down the tunnel to hell.

Through the wall's hole he hurtled, and then he *did* feel as if he were falling down a tunnel, for although his legs continued to run across a level surface, different geometries ruled this place—warps of time and space unlike those of the living world. The plunge got darker, darker. . . .

Dylan crashed into something he didn't expect. It seized him, this thing. Then it held him tightly in very strong arms.

They were the arms of a man Dylan never had seen before. A stranger's arms.

They wouldn't let go. Uncontrollably, like a trapped rabbit, Dylan trembled in their grip.

Frank Black tightened his hold on the shaking young man. "It's all right," he said soothingly. "I'm not going to hurt you. It's okay."

The kid didn't look so sure. Glassy-eyed, sweating, he stared at Frank as if beholding the devil himself. He seemed extremely confused, unable to think. Unable to talk, too. Maybe unable even to listen.

"Come on," Frank told him firmly. "Let's get out of here. You'd like to do that, wouldn't you?"

The kid continued to shake. Frank sensed profound terror; the effects of a powerful drug as well. Neither condition surprised him. Frank was certain that this guy had just recapitulated what Eedo Bolow had experienced in his final hours. A good chunk of what Bolow had gone through, that is. Luckily for this one, the process was being cut short. Frank glanced at the dim far recesses of the building's ceiling. Someone, or something, hid up there. A being whose party Frank had crashed. It really was time to go.

Frank wrapped a hand around the kid's left arm and half led, half dragged him toward the collapsed wall. After a few steps his resistance slackened. Frank didn't let go of the arm, however. Almost anything still could happen.

The kid might bolt, for instance. Then there remained the possibility, not so terribly far-fetched, that a wing-borne creature might choose to swoop.

They emerged from the factory. Frank marched his new charge across the pavement and down an alley to the inconspicuous spot where he had parked the car.

From Acme's roof—Through the night vision goggles—Watching—Watching grimly—With scorn— Watching the intruder hustle the kid away—

*However—Not ready to relinquish—No—
Not yet—*

Not yet—

Frank pulled into the SFPD garage and sig-
naled to the officer on duty that he needed
assistance. The slim woman approached, taking in the ashen-faced youth slumped on the
front seat. Taking in his blankly staring eyes,
the ribbon of drool trailing from his mouth.
The cuffs that restrained his hands.

"Book him?" the officer asked.

Frank shook his head. He studied the
woman's badge and said, "Observation room,
Officer Trent. Think we could use some coffee
up there. Along with Mike Atkins, Peter Watts,
Jim Penseyres. Ask the desk to make the calls?"

"Yeah," replied Trent, opening the passenger-side door. "Anything anybody needs to
know?"

Frank thought about that. "Yeah," he
said. "Watts should know that I found this
guy at Acme Dry Cleaning. In a state of distress."

Trent nodded. To the kid she said,
"C'mon, buddy. We got business upstairs."

The kid didn't move. He gave no sign he'd even heard words.

"In space," Trent remarked.

"Needs encouragement," Frank said wearily. "Good tug on the arm. I doubt he'll give trouble—but you might want . . ."

Trent pulled out her cell phone, pressed a speed-dial, and said, "Garage. Trent here. Got a zombie needs escorting."

The kid twitched.

"Signs of life," Trent said. "What's the name, my man?"

As before, she got no reply. Trent pursed her lips thoughtfully. Then with both hands she grabbed the kid's jacket and hauled him out of the car.

Frank crossed his arms on the steering wheel, making an ad hoc pillow for his suddenly aching head. What he'd done tonight was just beginning to sink in. He felt glad to be back here with himself and the kid intact. Relieved, actually, because he hadn't had a clue in advance about what he might find at Acme Dry Cleaning—and had proceeded to find more than he ever could have imagined. The BMWs. The gang of guys with short hair. The terrorization game with the victim. The victim rushing to his doom. Smacking into Frank instead.

All the while, a horrendously vile entity hovering in the rafters overhead ... Frank needed a break.

He parked the car, left the garage, and headed for a nearby diner that served undistracting fare.

Frank entered the observation room's viewing gallery forty minutes later. Mike Atkins stood there, staring through the big glass window at Watts and Penseyres seated at a table with the subject, questioning him. Frank saw at a glance that the interrogation wasn't going well. The subject looked sullen, blank. Watts asked him, voice tinny over the piped-in sound, "How long have you been in San Francisco?"

"I don't know," replied the kid. "What do you think?"

Penseyres said, "Come on. What were you doing out there tonight?"

"My name is Bob Smith," the kid muttered.

Frank turned to Atkins, handed him one of two plastic foam cups of coffee he'd brought in. "Anything?" he asked.

"Not yet," Atkins said dryly. "He's only

giving his name as Bob Smith." He gazed at the boy behind the glass and murmured, "He's saying we're talking to a dead man."

Frank offered no comment about that.

Atkins looked at him with questioning, penetrating eyes. He asked, "What were you doing out there, Frank?"

Frank said quietly, "I went back to satisfy a curiosity. About what happened there that night."

"And?" Atkins pressed.

Frank gazed through the glass at the kid, weighing his reply. "I think I know what he's afraid of," he said.

Atkins studied Frank's hooded eyes. Decisively he said, "Then maybe you should talk to him."

Frank took a deep breath and said, "Yeah."

A few minutes after Watts and Penseyres left the observation room, Frank went in. "Bob Smith" didn't meet his eyes. Frank took a seat at the table. The young man turned his chair to a wall, shoulders hunched. He didn't want to be here. He didn't want to talk.

Frank could deal with that. He stared. And waited.

Time passed. The object of Frank's attention became increasingly uncomfortable.

Frank finally said, "You've seen it, haven't you?"

The question elicited a slow turn of the boy's head.

"You've seen its hideous face," Frank continued. "Just like Eedo did. You've seen the red rain falling and the face of the beast."

Frank received a wary, frightened stare.

Behind the viewing gallery's one-way glass, Atkins, Watts, and Penseyres exchanged startled glances.

"I've seen it, too," Frank went on with soft matter-of-factness. "I know why you're afraid."

The kid stared at Frank with greater intensity. Frank locked eyes with him, engaging his own particular intensity.

Savaging Eedo . . . Mangling the face, shredding lips . . . Eedo's face horrified as the fangs hit . . . Red drizzle falling . . . And something else . . . Something new . . . A human figure . . . Intermittently, a human face . . .

Frank slipped from the vision, back to the pasty-faced boy in the observation room. He said, "You're safe from it now."

The kid's mouth slowly twisted into an

incredulous sneer. "No one is safe from it," he declared, a glow in his eyes mingling desperation with the certitude of a fanatic. "You don't know what you're talking about."

"How can it touch you here?" Frank asked.

The question elicited stony contempt.

"What can it *do* to you here?" Frank pressed on.

"You don't understand," the kid muttered, his face quivering. "It *knows*. It knows everything. It knows the numbers."

"What numbers?" Frank asked, his pulse quickening.

"That's all there is!" the kid exclaimed vehemently. "Phone numbers, serial numbers, card numbers—you and everybody else, the numbers are all we are! It knows your numbers and it knows *you*."

Frank pondered the outburst with growing astonishment. "What does it want?" he asked.

"Obedience," the kid blurted, a despairing throb in his voice. "Obedience and control."

Frank considered that. "In return for what?" he asked.

"To share in the power when the end comes," replied the kid. He grimaced, betraying deep hurt, regret. Anger. "When the everlasting fires rage in the Year of Destiny," he continued. "When the weak and the indolent perish."

Frank remained silent. He wanted more.

The kid released a broken sob; his eyes welled with tears. "They told me we were going to be *rich*," he said bitterly. "That we were the chosen ones. That discipline was the way to our own salvation. That prosperity was power." Tears streamed down his face. "They said we could leave whenever we wanted, but it was a lie. No one could leave. It made us turn on each other."

In his mind's eye Frank again glimpsed Eedo, writhing, thrashing. Blood-spattered . . .

The beast assaulting . . . The winged thing, descending like a raptor . . . Gnashing snout, the fangs . . . And yes, the human element . . . A face, wearing some kind of military hardware . . . Goggles . . . Night vision goggles . . . The human face blurs into the face of the beast again . . . vicious, greedy, gobbling . . . Relentless . . . A force before which ordinary human beings are helpless . . . Utterly hopeless . . .

Frank inhaled deeply. Although he knew the answer to his next question, he asked it anyway. "Did it kill Eedo Bolow?"

The kid nodded. "Yes," he said, a new

timbre in his voice, a note of finality, resignation; his eyes held an otherworldly glint. Slowly he said, "Because he was weak. Because he lost his discipline, just like the others did. Just like I did. Once you've lost your faith and discipline it will devour you. Nothing can save you from it."

Frank wanted to disagree. But the young man was radiating a seriousness that denied contradiction.

"You can't save me from it," the kid concluded, locking eyes with Frank again.

Frank noticed, however, that the eyes weren't focused on him. They were trained on him, yes; but they saw something beyond. Way beyond. A reality that neither Frank nor the observation room contained.

Then the guy who called himself Bob Smith turned away; as if suffering a seizure, his head shook. Frank noticed he'd stopped breathing, too. Two seconds passed. Still he held his breath.

Something was going very wrong. The boy's face reddened, his eyes bulged. In the neck, veins stood out like cords.

Frank leapt to his feet and grabbed the kid's shoulders; they felt rigid, paralyzed. The jaw was clenched, the mouth tightly compressed. The eyes stared fixedly into some distant place. A place they'd do well to avoid . . .

"Hey!" Frank shouted, easing the stiffened body to the floor.

Atkins, Watts, and Penseyres burst into the room. "Get a doctor," Atkins snapped. Penseyres rushed out.

Frank tried to pry open the mouth. He couldn't; it felt like carved stone. Feverishly he loosened the kid's shirt and started administering CPR.

Watts leaned down, took the boy's head in his hands. "Holy hell," he muttered. "What got into him?"

Frank whaled away on the chest with flattened palms, his face taut with focus, as if through sheer will forcing life into the rigidifying body. "C'mon!" he bellowed. "Breathe!"

But Bob Smith wouldn't breathe. His eyes rolled back, revealing dull whites. Sputum dribbled from his mouth. The head listed, limp.

"No!" Frank shouted. "*Don't die!*"

"Frank," Watts said sharply.

Still Frank pressed into the chest.

"Frank!" Watts exclaimed.

"Oh my God," Frank muttered. "Oh my God."

"He's dead, Frank," Watts said. "Dead."

Frank stared at the corpse with disbelief. "I lost him," he whispered. "I saved him. And lost him."

Watts pulled Frank to his feet. "Let's go," he said somberly. "You did what you could."

MILLENNIUM
CHAPTER
17

The next morning Frank went for a walk in Victory Park, San Francisco's memorial to veterans lost to war. It was a bright, cheerful day, nearly cloudless. The city hummed and honked with the usual A.M. bustle: briskly striding businesspeople, kids on bikes, ambling tourists, buses, more buses, the riverine ebb and flow of traffic.

Frank paused at the park's tall obelisk monument. He gazed at the four flags of the armed service branches, at the U.S. flag fluttering in the center. Insignia of duty to country; insignia of sacrifice. Of honor. Of ashes.

A meeting was scheduled to take place here soon. At the moment, though, Frank felt content to be alone with his thoughts. For several minutes he contemplated the monument. In the far background, a construction crane rose starkly against the sky, a reminder of life's continuity in the shadow of the dead.

"Go home, Frank," said a familiar voice.

Frank turned to snowy-haired Mike Atkins. The man was regarding him with kindly concern, coupled with the fierce and almost paternal authority that Frank had come to welcome from this colleague. This very dear friend.

"I think you should go home," Atkins continued, "and see your family. And get some rest."

Frank's face betrayed what was haunting him. He muttered, "That kid died of fright, Mike."

"He was so full of LSD we'll never know what he died of," Atkins replied.

"He couldn't escape it," Frank murmured wonderingly. "Whatever it was . . . what could be so powerful that you couldn't escape it?"

Atkins said testily, "What you described in there last night—the face of the beast . . ."

"I saw it," Frank declared in a low voice

that mixed mystification with certitude. "The day I arrived."

To which Atkins declared, "I've seen the face of evil, Frank. I've looked into its eyes and seen it staring back at me. But the face has always been a man's face. A human face."

Frank remained silent. This wasn't a topic he chose to debate right now.

"I've always believed," Atkins went on, "that evil is born in a cold heart and a weak mind."

"I have, too," Frank said simply.

The two men gazed at each other. Neither had access to words that could describe what they'd been confronting the previous several days. But in each other's eyes they found re-acknowledgment of a central fact:

This case was like nothing they'd ever seen before.

A few hours later Frank was back at home on his long metal ladder, adjusting the new security light, intent on preventing false alarms.

"Hey there, Frank!" piped the insistent voice of Jack Meredith.

Frank looked down at his neighbor's broad face. As usual, it was beaming with cheer, and unquenchable curiosity.

"See you were gone for a few days, huh?" Meredith inquired, his voice probingly high-pitched. "Work?"

"Hi, Jack," Frank said patiently. "Yeah. Work."

"Working with that consulting group you mentioned?"

"Yeah."

"Consulting," Meredith said. "That's one of those *things*. You always wonder what exactly that means, y'know . . ."

"Well," said Frank, descending the ladder, "basically we're given a problem. And we try to solve it."

"Oh, I see," Meredith said avidly. "So— did you solve the problem you were working on, Frank?"

Frank gazed at Meredith for several long moments. "No," he said, his eyes clouding, the formulation of a reply taking him elsewhere. "No, I didn't solve it, Jack. I couldn't make sense of it."

"Gee," said Meredith, his eyes widening.

Frank looked away.

Even Jack Meredith could tell that this conversation would go no further. "Well, I'll see you, Frank."

Frank smiled vacantly. "Yeah. You will, Jack."

That night, getting on toward bedtime, Frank found himself occupied with some reading material he hadn't consulted for quite a while. He sat on the edge of his bed, dressed in the usual sweatpants and T-shirt nightgear, thin-rimmed glasses perched on his nose. A hefty book lay in his lap. The Christian Holy Bible.

In Ephesians, Chapter Six, Verse Twelve, he found a passage that caught his eye:

"The rulers of the darkness of this world are contending for mastery over the bodies and minds of all members of the human race."

Frank pondered the meaning of the passage. Then he flipped back to a passage he'd consulted earlier, in the Book of Matthew. Chapter Twenty-five, Verse Forty-one read:

"Depart from Me, ye cursed, into everlasting fire, prepared for the devil and his angels."

The words seemed to reach out to Frank, demand his attention.

Catherine entered the bedroom, bathrobe-clad. "Did you want to say good night to Jordan?" she asked.

"Yeah," Frank replied, setting the Bible aside.

Catherine took note of the title on the book's now-exposed cover. "I hear it's a real potboiler," she remarked. "Full of treachery, death, violence . . ."

Absentmindedly Frank nodded. "Yeah," he agreed, a rote smile turning up the corners of his mouth.

"Looking for moral guidance?" Catherine inquired sweetly. "Or just a little light bed-time reading?"

Frank shrugged. "Some answers, I guess," he replied, his features guarded, moody. "Something that happened down in San Francisco."

"Anything you want to talk about?" Catherine asked.

"I'm just confused about something I thought I understood," Frank said. "Evil. What it is exactly."

"You mean what causes it?" Catherine said, sitting beside Frank on the bed.

Frank nodded and said, "It seems the old

biblical concept of the devil's influence has lost any currency."

Catherine thought about that. "I just think the language has changed," she commented. "I think science and psychology have given us a clearer idea of why people commit evil acts." She sighed. "I see it every day in my job. Abused kids become abusive adults."

Frank glanced at her. "So the true source of evil is us," he said, his tone conveying a trace of doubt.

"You mean are we all capable of it?" Catherine asked.

Frank didn't seem to register the question. "Or is there something out there," he went on gravely. "A force or a presence. Waiting. Until it can create another murder, another rape. Another Holocaust."

Catherine blinked. In a deliberative tone that acknowledged the weight of Frank's concerns, she said, "I think it's something everyone who looks deeply at life wonders."

Frank gazed at her, troubled. "What would you tell a child? What would I tell Jordan?"

For an instant, worry crossed Catherine's face. Then she brightened and said soothingly, "Maybe you should just tell her good night."

Frank raised his eyebrows. His wife's down-to-earth guidance appealed to him. Grateful for it, he went to Catherine and gave her a tender kiss.

Jordan was asleep when Frank entered her room. But she smiled when Frank leaned down to move her from the bed's edge, pull the covers up to her chin. He rose and stood over her, not quite ready to leave, gazing at his daughter's peaceful face. The sight inspired the first delight, and unreserved smile, he'd experienced in too long a time.

Minutes later Frank switched on the light in his basement office, and activated his computer.

Idle speculation hadn't prompted the Bible study. Frank couldn't let go of the mystery in San Francisco. He needed answers, and was going to do his best to find them.

While the machine booted up he pulled his dictionary from a shelf, flipped through the G's. For the word *Gehenna* he found this definition:

"1. (in the New Testament) hell; 2. a place of burning, torment, or misery."

The computer screen lit up with a menu.

Frank tapped his keyboard, accessed SearchNet, and typed in GEHENNA.

The phone rang. Slightly startled, Frank checked his watch. Calls at this hour were unusual.

"Hello," he said into the phone's mouthpiece.

"Frank, it's Mike Atkins," said the man with whom Frank had conversed that morning in San Francisco's Victory Park. "I'm sorry to be calling so late."

"I'm up working anyway," Frank remarked.

"So am I," Atkins said.

"Where are you?" Frank asked.

"I'm still in San Francisco, at the forensics lab," Atkins said, his voice tense. "We got data back on the dead boy earlier tonight. Found something we weren't expecting."

"What?" Frank said, swiveling his chair.

"The kid's clothing and tissue showed traces of an insecticide used in the making of something called sarin."

Frank said quietly, "Sarin gas."

"Which was used in the terrorist attack on the subway in Japan. The leader of the cult believed to be responsible is on trial for that attack, as well as for several other murders."

"Shoko Asahara," Frank said, recalling the case. "Leader of the Aum Shinrikyo."

"That's right," Atkins said. "'Supreme Truth' is the closest translation of the cult's name. Frank, do you know how they say Asahara disposed of his victims?"

Frank frowned, his mind suddenly on point. He muttered, "In an industrial scale microwave . . ."

Eedo pounding the glass . . . His agonized face pressed against the glass . . . His hand going limp, sliding . . . His head dropping from view . . .

Frank typed commands on his keyboard, his heart now thudding.

Atkins was saying, "Asahara had amassed over a billion dollars. He'd been trying to buy weapons from the Russians. They think he may even have been trying to get ahold of the Ebola virus."

"He wanted to bring on Armageddon," Frank said.

"Could it happen here, Frank?" Atkins demanded.

Frank didn't know. But the possibility electrified him. So did the Internet listing that was scrolling down his computer screen. The last entry read:

GEHENNA INTERNATIONAL, PTY.
REG CAYMAN ISLANDS. INDUSTRIAL
CHEMICAL HOLDINGS.

NEW YORK, MONACO, SAN
FRANCISCO, TOKYO, SYDNEY, CAIRO.
STORAGE PLANTS.

"Frank?" Atkins said. "You there?"

"Listen, Mike," Frank said with sudden
urgency. I just found something. There's a
business listing for a Gehenna International.
It looks like some kind of offshore holding
company."

"What do they deal in?" Atkins asked.

"Industrial products, chemicals," Frank
replied, working his keyboard. "Mike, they
list one of their plants in San Francisco."

For a fraction of second, stunned silence
came over the line. Then Atkins snapped,
"I'm on it."

The connection clicked off. Slowly Frank set
down his phone. He stared at the screen, thinking about his find. About Mike Atkins looking
into it . . . Frank suddenly felt extremely uneasy.
He picked up his phone again, rapidly punched
in the number for the SFPD forensics lab, and listened to several long rings. Unanswered rings.

Atkins, evidently, already was out the
door.

Frank slammed down the phone, leapt to
his feet, and ran up two flights of stairs to the
hallway outside his and Catherine's bedroom.

He went through the doorway and paused, his body taut, coiled like a spring.

Catherine, sitting in bed reading, gave him a bemused look. "What?" she said.

"I don't know," Frank muttered, coming in the room. "I just have a very bad feeling about something."

He went to the bedside phone, picked it up, and called San Francisco. Somehow he knew that Atkins would encounter trouble at Gehenna International. The dictionary definition throbbed in his mind:

A *place of burning, torment, or misery.*

Catherine stared at Frank with rising alarm.

MILLENNIUM
CHAPTER
18

Rain fell in sheets from the dark skies over San Francisco, rendering an industrial district on the outskirts of town more desolate than it otherwise would have been. Mike Atkins had never driven through the area before. He'd made his way here with the aid of a map and an address for Gehenna International, Pty.

The factory complex to which the address belonged consisted of several large interconnected buildings. No lights burned in them, or anywhere around them; Atkins saw no signage, either. The establishment's anonymity struck him as a little odd. But then, thousands of such complexes existed throughout industrial America, for one reason or another not inclined to advertise their identities, their purposes. Classified government projects, the presence of sensitive materials, security and public relations—dozens of issues could motivate management to keep a low profile.

The production of sarin gas, for example.

Twelve people had been killed and more than six thousand badly injured in the Tokyo subway attack during the morning rush hour of March 20, 1995. Large though the toll was, it would have been immensely bigger had the doomsday cult's scientists prepared a purer form of sarin. And it was anyone's guess what damage Aum Shinrikyo might have inflicted if it had used even a fraction of its other resources. Two years later, fresh revelations continued to be made concerning a remote ranch in Australia that the cult had owned, which just so happened to have been located near an enormous and mysterious explosion that some experts believed to be nuclear. Officials insisted a meteorite caused the blast; Atkins had doubts about that explanation.

A tall chain-link fence surrounded the

Gehenna complex. Atkins parked by a gate
that proved, somewhat to his surprise, to be
unlocked. He moved through it with a lit
flashlight, ignoring the rain pouring down.
Moisture was the least of his concerns right
now. Guards, and alarms, occupied his mind's
center court.

But he encountered neither. Who, or
what, kept an eye on this place?

Perhaps nothing did. A side entry was in
fact locked, but only cursorily. Atkins picked
it in less than a minute.

The entry led to a long, pitch-dark hallway. Atkins probed with his flashlight. Like
the building's exterior, the hallway was plain,
bare. Just about empty, actually.

Midway down the hall, Atkins opened a
door and discovered the first evidence of
organized activity. A large room was devoid
of people, but held row upon row of tables
and chairs. Work stations of some kind. All
the chairs faced in the same direction; before
each one sat a telephone.

At the room's other end, positioned for
easy viewing from the chairs, stood a large
video monitor. The machine was lit. As
Atkins stared at it, words came onscreen:

FACILITATE ENVY

Atkins's mind raced. He recalled "Bob Smith's" feverish comments about "the numbers." Credit card numbers, among others. This is a boiler room, Atkins realized. A place where people pitched sales over the phone.

The words on the video monitor changed to:

WORK WILL SET YOU FREE

Atkins wondered who or what was operating the video system. And why. Were the slogans being displayed for his benefit? They certainly weren't directed to the absent occupants of all these chairs.

Uneasily he glanced around. Still no sign of any human presence. Objects mounted in the ceiling caught his eye: three mirrored hemispheres, placed at intervals along the length of the room. Atkins identified them as video surveillance pods. Eyes-in-the-sky. Might they be operational this very minute? Within the closest one, an element glowed.

Through the video surveillance system—Watching a screen—Watching the white-haired man stare directly into a camera—Watching unease mount on his face—Apprehension—

The first stirrings of fear—

Atkins decided to move on, investigate a bit further what the complex harbored. Why not? So far, no one was stopping him. He walked back to the hallway, went all the way down it, and followed a covered outdoor walkway to a large adjoining building. A warehouse, from the look of it.

That the building was. It comprised a single huge room filled with stacks of product on wooden pallets. Extensive metal shelvings, crammed with goods, partitioned much of the space into a maze of aisles. Atkins couldn't begin make out the extent of the materials stored here. But one thing was clear. He'd happened across a sizable depot.

Down an aisle he moved, using his flashlight to pick out details. A cluster of large steel drums caught his attention. In big letters, they were marked FLAMMABLE. Smaller letters spelled SODIUM FLUORIDE—a chemical used in the manufacture of insecticide. And sarin gas.

Ahead, wooden crates sitting in shelves aroused his curiosity. They bore Chinese characters and markings, and the words REPUBLIC OF CHINA. A prybar lay on a shelf; Atkins used it to pry open one of the lids. The job required some work; sweat began to mix with the residue of rain on his face. He got the lid off. Underneath lay long packages

wrapped in brown craft paper. Atkins caught
a whiff of metal-scented oil; he knew this
smell. To confirm what he strongly suspected,
he slit the paper. Yes, just as he'd thought—
his flashlight beam gleamed on the barrel of a
brand new AK-47 combat rifle.

What else was stashed here? Atkins
moved on.

An armada of SFPD squad cars, seven plain-
wraps and five black and whites, raced
through the night. The sirens weren't on, but
whirling rooftop light bars thrashed through
the rainy air, clearing traffic from the roads
ahead.

Peter Watts and Jim Penseyres sat in the
rear seat of the lead car, edgy, impatient. They
didn't know what to expect at the business
enterprise named Gehenna International—for
this emergency rush to it hadn't been mobilized
by information of a solid nature. Something
more compelling had accomplished that:

A phone call from Seattle. The urgency
in Frank Black's voice.

◄O►   ◄O►   ◄O►

Atkins turned a corner in the warehouse labyrinth. His flashlight beam swept across a large metallic cube thirty feet ahead. A heavy door, about six feet tall and slightly ajar, gave access to the thing, which looked to be a machine of some kind. The door held a thick glass window, a viewing port. Atkins advanced on it.

He realized that the machine was a jumbo ventilated oven. An industrial microwave, in fact.

Flashlight extended, he peered inside. The interior went six feet deep. In the rearmost area lay a mound of a whitish powdery substance, from which extruded objects that appeared more solid.

Ashes, Atkins thought with horror. *Fragments of bone.*

Something had abraded the oven's interior wall directly to his right. The surface was scored there, worn down; so too was the inside of the door just below the window. Scratch marks! Atkins speculated grimly. The product of desperate pounding?

The cavalcade of police cars tore up to the Gehenna complex and came to a screeching halt. Watts and Penseyres led a scramble of officers through the gate and into the side door. Down the dark hallway they ran, flashlights finding no trace of Atkins, indeed of anyone, in various rooms off the hallway. Watts shouted, "The next building, come on, come on!"

Atkins moved inside the oven, knelt to more closely examine the apparent bones to the rear. There was a good deal of the stuff on the floor. . . .

Behind him, the massive door slammed shut.

Atkins whirled, hurled his shoulder against the door. It wouldn't budge. "Hey!" he shouted. "Hey!" He continued to pound the door—it was locked, he realized, locked from the outside. He then realized that he was pounding the very area of the door that others had pounded before.

A loud hum filled the oven, and bright light as well. The machine *was going into operation*—Atkins stopped pounding, incredulous that this actually could be happening to him. He felt a blast of heat radiation penetrate him deeply; his eyes widened with terror.

Then he saw a dark figure beyond the thick glass window. A man, standing there. Staring through night vision goggles.

Atkins beat on the window with all his might, bellowing from the bottom of his lungs.

Watts burst through the covered walkway into the warehouse. To the rear of the enormous shadowy space, he heard a loud hum. Shouting encouragement, he led Penseyres and the other men toward it. He rounded a corner and saw the big metal cube, the brightly glowing window in its door. "Turn it off!" he yelled as he realized what the humming machine had to be. He bolted to it. He seized the handle and turned, but the handle wouldn't give; then it did and the door swung open.

Atkins lay in a heap on the oven's floor, his face white, his hair a sweaty aureole, steam rising from his clothes.

"Get an ambulance!" Penseyres shouted amid the babble of horror and confusion spreading through the men. "Do it now!"

Penseyres and Watts dragged the body out of the oven.

"Are we too late?" Penseyres asked anxiously.

"Don't know," Watts muttered, leaning over to find a pulse. Atkins's wrist was scalding hot.

Watts couldn't find a pulse. Maybe a faint trace of one—very faint.

Behind him, the officer in charge issued terse orders to his personnel: Fan through the complex and secure the place. Then he radioed for backup. Lots of it.

"Mike," Watts said with feeling to his limp mentor and friend. "Hold on, Mike. Help's coming, buddy. Hold on."

MILLENNIUM
CHAPTER

19

Frank didn't waste time trying to rent a car this late at night at San Francisco International. He got directly into a cab.

The hospital was his primary destination. First, though, he would make a stop at SFPD headquarters. The police had taken into custody an individual he wanted to check out.

Rain lashed the cab's windows, providing little relief from Frank's preoccupations: Mike Atkins. The unspeakable thing that had happened to him. The unspeakable entity responsible.

The cab stopped a block from the SFPD, unable to get closer because of TV news trucks clogging the street. Frank paid the fare, loped the block, and used a back entrance.

In the second-floor corridor outside the observation/interrogation room, a wall monitor was tuned to news. The anchor was saying solemnly, "San Francisco law enforcement agencies worked in tense cooperation in the roundup and arrest of what is being referred to as a 'death cult,' whose aim is believed to be nothing less than mass destruction."

Frank paused to watch footage of young, short-haired, handcuffed men being taken to police vehicles. Among the prisoners was an older man, grim-faced, sallow-complexioned. The anchor was saying, "The suspected leader is a former chemical engineer named Ricardo Clenett. He is being held on suspicion of the murder of at least one cult member." Frank stared at the man's video image; in his stomach, a knot of dread tightened. "Authorities confiscated a large cache of chemical and biological weapons purchased on the global black market," the anchor continued. "Funded by . . ."

Frank pushed into the observation room's viewing gallery. No one was there. Beyond the one-way window, however, an interrogation was in progress.

Peter Watts, leaning over the table with his hands flattened on its surface, was questioning Ricardo Clenett.

"How many boys died in there?" Watts demanded. "How many kids did you send to their deaths? Ten? *Twenty?*"

Clenett ignored Watts.

Frank went closer to the window. His gaunt, haunted face reflected from the glass; the image seemed to hover midair next to the prisoner, who stared impassively past Watts, as if Peter weren't even in the room.

Watts slammed a hand on the interrogation table and bellowed, *"What the hell are you?"*

Clenett's face showed not the slightest reaction.

Disgusted, Watts left the room. Moments later he joined Frank in the viewing gallery. "Nothing," he muttered. "Absolutely nothing."

"I think I know," Frank said quietly.

"What?" Watts said.

"Who he is," Frank whispered.

As if aware of Frank, aware of the lined face and burning eyes reflecting in the viewing gallery's window, Clenett rose from the table, went to the window, and stared through the mirrored surface it presented to him.

Directly at Frank.

Clenett's pockmarked face had a sealed quality. A quality of containment—as if the face were a force field. It held back something ferocious. Something explosive. This man's spirit looked to have been laminated so thoroughly that nothing could penetrate it.

But plenty could suffer from it. As plenty had.

Frank muttered, "I've got to get out of here, Peter." He left the room.

At the hospital, in Mike Atkins's room, Frank occupied a chair next to the plastic-tented bed, staring bleakly into space. He'd been here for hours. He had no intention of leaving anytime soon.

Under the clear tent Mike's face held an unnaturally glistening pallor. He was alive, though. Just barely.

The door opened. Jim Penseyres poked his head through and said, "Your wife's here."

Catherine stood behind Penseyres, looking at her husband with quiet concern. Frank brightened minutely. He rose, went through the door. Penseyres entered the room and took Frank's bedside station.

Frank closed the door and said to Catherine, "You didn't have to come."

"I wanted to be here," Catherine said tenderly. "I wanted to be here with you, Frank." She touched his arm and added, "I know it's what you fear."

"What?" Frank said.

"Losing control," replied Catherine. Frank met her eyes and held them, acknowledging the truth of her words as she added, "Having something like this happen to someone you care about."

Frank looked away. "He had serious internal cellular damage from the radiation," he said hollowly. "But the doctors say he's going to pull through."

"I know," Catherine said. "And he will."

Frank nodded.

"I know you know this," Catherine went on, striving to reach Frank, comfort him. "How many other lives you may have saved. How many people could have been hurt by those weapons."

Frank looked away again, bleakness returning to his face, hooding his eyes. "I know," he said without conviction.

Catherine moved closer and took his hands. "What you did was important," she said, her voice calm, soothing. "You did what you set out to do, Frank." She squeezed his hands and declared softly, "You caught the bad man."

"I'm not sure," Frank muttered, giving his wife a brief glance.

"Not sure of what?" Catherine asked.

"Not sure . . ." Frank murmured. Again he glanced at Catherine, and again he turned away, his eyebrows knitting. "Not sure," he finally said, "if the bad man can be caught."

Catherine considered the statement, her eyes filling with concern. And then, with understanding.

Frank put his arms around her. They hugged tightly, for the moment joined, completing each other, their embrace removing them from the harshly lit hospital corridor, from this place of cold facts and final uncertainties. Taking them away, for the moment, from the suffering. From the horror.

Be sure to look for

MILLENNIUM

WEEDS

BY
VICTOR KOMAN

BASED ON THE CHARACTERS
CREATED BY
CHRIS CARTER

SCREENPLAY BY
FRANK SPOTNITZ

Coming from HarperPrism

MILLENNIUM
PROLOGUE

Safety is an illusion. There is no safe place. He knows this now. Fences, gates, walls, locks; these do nothing to keep out an enemy already within. Corpses rot from the inside out. Weeds grow beneath perfectly trimmed lawns only to burst forth and ruin beauty.

The corruption that lurks within seeming perfection haunts his nights and his days. Mottled, decaying flesh and hollowed, dying eyes everywhere mock him. And only an ocean of blood can purify this evil place. Nothing but blood.

Cold blood.

Pure blood.

MILLENNIUM
═══════════════
CHAPTER
═══════════════

A weed growing through a crack in an otherwise gray and perfect square of sidewalk glistened with late-afternoon mist from the cloud-scattered January sky. A few yards away whirled the nylon dervish of an electric weed whacker closing in on its prey— one of the few weeds of winter. The faint scent of ozone mingled with the smells of supper cooking in dozens of kitchens on the block and the sharp tang of freshly slaughtered garden invaders.

The whipping tendrils slashed at the

offensive, thick-stemmed weed, dismembering it and flinging its remains to the breeze.

The driver in the van watched it die.

He gazed at the middle-aged man operating the weed trimmer, then shifted his attention to the children at play on the man's lawn. The street—one of the nicer ones in Vista Verde Estates—bustled with late-Sunday activity: a boy in a sky blue sweatshirt and a girl in a red-checked Pendleton threw a ball back and forth on a manicured lawn, its grass dormant this late in the year and covered with patches of snow displaying the remnants of snow angels; cars returned from day-trips, families enjoying the good life.

He knew better.

From within his late-model dark blue minivan, he observed the two-story homes flanking the street, canary red mailboxes standing at attention like toy soldiers. Vista Verde Estates looked safe, tranquil, pure. The music on his tape deck—Ferrante and Teicher—should have made the world bright and beautiful.

He knows otherwise.

The gardener stares up at the van, unable to see within. From inside, though, the driver sees the snow-tinged lawn turn black and foul. His nostrils fill with the cloying scent of rotting grass. The houses on the block drip blood-red. The sky itself drains of color, turning dark, ominous, and black as slate.

He drives slowly through this demonic realm, searching. He stares in alarm at the children. Their figures move like wraiths, haunted and defiled. They stare with dead eyes from faces little more than pocked, decaying flesh. The gardening man gazes once more at the van, this time with black, hollow sockets.

A wretched taste fills the driver's mouth with the sharp, salty flavor of blood. The air smells of mildew, vomit, burning rubber, excrement. His head aches, his eyes burn.

He pulls over beneath the shelter of a large tree, glancing in his side-view mirror to ensure that he parks straight and close to the curb. The dark tint of the minivan windows hides him from the creatures outside as he buries his face in his hands. Despair surges through him with the force of a monstrous sea storm. He weeps uncontrollably for a long while.

Deep breaths, rapid and cleansing, calm him. Then he looks up again at the bright boughs of the evergreen tree. . . .

And sees only charcoal black, twisted

limbs against roiling liquid storm clouds obliterating a lifeless death-shroud sky. Lightning bolts flash like heavenly retribution blasting a world horrifyingly in need of cleansing.

"'But know ye for certain,'" he whispers hoarsely over a tongue numbed by the blood and death he tastes. "'Ye shall surely bring innocent blood upon yourselves and upon this city, and upon the inhabitants thereof. . . . .'"

MILLENNIUM

CHAPTER

2

J osh Comstock watched the candles flickering on the cake as his mother carried it from the kitchen to the den. She smiled, auburn hair a little duller than he remembered but still more or less in possession of the cheerleader prettiness he had seen in her high school photographs. Setting the cake down in front of him to the sound of the Happy Birthday Song, she wafted the familiar scents of perfume, chocolate cake, and burning candle wax toward him.

Fifteen times he had gone through this

before, and this was the most uncomfortable he had ever felt. He greeted the presentation with a sullen stare, brushing his long blond hair behind his ears and gazing at the flaming wicks before him.

The song ended. With a sigh, he looked around him, nodded, and blew out the red-blue-yellow-pink candles. Gunmetal-gray smoke curled up from the extinguished glow like a ghost.

Cheers. Pats on the back from relatives. Nothing in their gaiety could cheer him.

Mrs. Petey, wife of the homeowner association president, pulled out the candle stumps. She was in her thirties, sported a blond perm, was probably ten years younger than his own mom, and always had a smile for him, though lately the smile seemed as forced as his mother's. As artificial as those on a lot of people around here.

"Sixteen," she said with joyful amazement. "You're practically a man now, Josh."

"Yeah." Josh felt no enthusiasm for the milestone. Reaching for a knife, he raised it slowly upward, then brought it down against the soft blue and white frosting, pressing into the cake with quiet disinterest.

A screen door slammed suddenly. "Where's my son?" cried a strong, masculine voice. "Aha, there he is!"

Josh's father pushed through the crowd surrounding his son. With a businessman's good looks, slightly gray at the temples, blue eyes behind wire-rimmed glasses, he beamed at his son as if Josh were six instead of sixteen and he had brought home a pony for the boy. He shoved aside some of the big blue balloons.

"Sorry I'm late," he said. "Josh, Can you come out here? I have something to show you." He stepped back outside as the party guests—smiling—cleared a path for Josh to walk into the backyard. He turned his head to say, "We'll be right back, folks."

There on the grass sat a new Vector MX motorcycle, with red tank, blue saddle, and white plastic armor. His dad stood proudly beside it as the party guests murmured, impressed.

It looked great. Sleek. Fast. Probably burn up the streets in this sleepy, gated community. He desperately wanted to jump on it and roar away. Right now. Without having to thank anyone, least of all his dad. He walked toward it, nodding, trying to show neither his excitement nor his secret belief that the gift was a bribe.

His dad's smile lost some of its intensity. "You like it?"

Josh ran a hand along the tank, still nodding.

"It's cool," he said noncommittally. "I'm gonna take it out."

His dad smiled. "Just be home by curfew."

Josh slipped the new dark, wine-hued helmet off the handlebars and strapped it on. Throwing a leg over the saddle, he slid on and thumbed the starter. The engine roared to life and throbbed under his thighs, the hot scent of exhaust filling his lungs. Heeling the kickstand up, he paused to glance at his parents before he rode away.

Josh's dad smiled at his wife, but the look she returned her husband betrayed a dark emotion that Josh could only guess about. He felt he could make a pretty good guess, though. He did not think she actually knew the secret he and his father shared, but he knew that she must have her suspicions.

He maneuvered the motorcycle into the street and gunned it, oblivious to the nondescript minivan under the shady tree that suddenly eased into life, pulling out to follow Josh away from the warm lights of his home.

MILLENNIUM
CHAPTER

S treet lamps flickered on as Josh Comstock raced the day into darkness. Vista Verde Estates still had several phases of construction left. One halfway-completed cul-de-sac a few blocks away served as Josh's personal proving ground for the bike. He tried a few tight turns, sprayed up a rooster tail of construction dirt and loose gravel, laid the bike down once without any apparent damage, and got back up on the metal stallion for more.

With a roar, he sped up a small incline of earth and launched a couple of feet into the air, landing straight and firm. He finished off with a tight turn that flung weeds and icy mud in a three-quarter circle around his pivoting front wheel.

The driver of the minivan saw it all as he pulled to a stop under a streetlight. The high-pressure sodium vapor lamp still glowed a dull pink, heating up for its nightly duty. It flickered between pink and its hot-peach full-power level a few times, then snapped up to bright. Harsh shadows created a landscape of black and gray. Pools of midnight amid islands of barely any light at all.

He set the minivan's brake and slipped the transmission into park. Without shutting off the engine, he reached for his flashlight, a sleek, black, four-cell aluminum-body style, and another black baton with twin stainless steel tips on the business end. The cold metal felt like a sword in his hand.

Climbing quickly out of the van, he walked purposefully across the damp pavement toward the other side of the cul-de-sac, flashlight in one hand, baton in the other. The cold night air numbed his lungs with the scent of pine and damp earth. His black-and-white running shoes made soft, squishing sounds against the slickened asphalt, totally obscured by the angry-bee buzz of Josh Comstock's motorcycle.

The Comstock boy skidded to a halt upon seeing the bobbing white beam aimed in his direction. Squinting and holding up a hand toward the relentlessly approaching man, he tried to peer past the glare, then said loudly, placatingly, "Hey, it's Okay! I-I'm going home right now!"

The driver raised the baton and thrust it toward Josh. As if shot, he jerked backward off the bike and fell to the muddy ground, staring up with sudden terror. It was the look a mortal would give upon seeing an avenging angel, the driver thought, just before the vision overcame him once more.

The boy lays on the ground, speechless and writhing. He is not a boy, though. An ancient, corrupted face contorts in a miserable, uncomprehending grimace.

The smell of ozone and singed flesh strikes his nostrils as he lunges the cattle prod again and again at the quivering, prostrate monstrosity down in the slime. He subdues the boy and feels an overwhelming relief. The salty taste in his mouth subsides, the rapid beating of his heart begins to slow, and his fierce breathing abates. He knows what he must do to the Comstock boy, for his own good.

Only blood will cure this evil, come the words in his head. *Only blood*.

MILLENNIUM
CHAPTER
4

The digital green of the alarm clock readout battled with morning light and only barely won. The time turned from six fifty-nine A.M. to seven A.M. and brought with it a raucous buzz. Linda Comstock reached out her hand and wearily slapped the device into silence.

The morning tasted pretty rotten to her as she rolled out of her side of the bed and reached for her robe and slippers. She ignored her husband lying with his back to her. She could tell when he lay there awake,

pretending to be asleep. His whole body gave
off tense vibes. He did not fake the natural
way she knew he slept. How could he?
He was never able to observe it firsthand, the
way she had for their twenty years of marriage.

She padded down the hall in her slippers,
coming to Josh's bedroom door. It hung
slightly ajar, so she knocked softly.

"Josh?" she whispered. Her nose wrinkled
at an unusual smell from his room. Something coppery, mixed in with an outhouse
odor of urine and excrement. Muscles tensing
involuntarily, she fought back maternal fears
as just another false alarm in so many years of
fearing for her son. It was that fear that had
brought them to Vista Verde to wall them-
selves inside a safe community.

The door opened on well-lubricated
hinges. As she flung the drapes back to let in
daylight, she saw a form lying under the rum-
pled sheets.

"I don't know how late you were running
around last night—"

She stood over him, smelling the acrid
odor, feeling her heart pound in near panic.
Then she saw the sickening stain of red that
drenched the top sheet.

"Josh?"

He lay utterly motionless, the deep burgundy motorcycle helmet still on his head.

In a single motion she ripped the covers from him to see more blood soaking the sheets. Blood everywhere. Most of all, blood at the end of his leather-jacketed arms, gnawed stumps where hands should have been.

With a cry of utter anguish that brought her husband bursting into the room, she pulled the helmet from the lifeless head on the pillow.

And saw a dead teenage boy who was not Josh. A dead boy with red-brown-black blood drenching his mouth and chin.

"That's not my son!" she shrieked.

Relieved, then suddenly even more terrified, she stared at the olive-skinned body with the raven hair and cried in baffled fear and rage, "Oh, my God! That's not my son!"

LEWIS GANNETT was born in Washington, D.C., grew up in Europe, went to Harvard and the Massachusetts Institute of Technology, dropped out to become a waiter, then started writing. He is the author of *The Living One* and *Magazine Beach*.